THE PASSION OF FRANKENSTEIN

THE PASSION OF FRANKENSTEIN

A Continuation of Mary Shelley's Novel

MARVIN KAYE

WILDSIDE PRESS

Published by Wildside Press, LLC
www.wildsidebooks.com

To

My Dear Friend, Colleague,

Frankensteinian Devotee,

& Holmesian Par Excellence,

CAROLE BUGGÉ

a/k/a C. E. Lawrence

from

Your Devoted Watson

CONTENTS

PART THREE
At Dunkeld Cathedral

EPILOGUE

PROLOGUE

Epistolary

*From Mrs. Margaret Saville, England
to Mr. Ernest Frankenstein, of Geneva*

7 March

MY DEAR SIR,

In a letter of introduction that I posted last spring, I told you how it came to be that I, a stranger, learned of the fate of your poor tormented brother Victor Frankenstein, who perished in the region of the Arctic Circle despite the efforts of my own sibling, Captain R. Walton, to nurse him back to health.

At my brother's last posting, I was pleased and relieved to learn that he had very reluctantly agreed to turn his vessel south toward England and safety.

Judge of my wonder and dismay when last week I received a new letter that I found rife with new horror. At my brother's suggestion, I have employed our village clerk to render a true copy for your perusal.

Mrs. M. Saville

From Capt. R. Walton
To Mrs. Saville, England

November 13th

MY DEAR SISTER,

I supposed that my adventures were now at an end, and tried to console myself that, at least, I should soon behold your dear face and the verdant Cotswolds, but Fate has visited new strife upon my ship and its hapless crew. Yet do be reassured, for intervention unlikely and strange has rescued me from an obscure Arctic grave.

If these messages have arrived out of sequence, you will not understand what I am about to tell you, so it is meet that I shall briefly recapitulate my preceding letter, which introduced a pair of quite remarkable personages and described a series of unusual (perhaps I should say bizarre) events that commenced some months ago.

At that time, after we had sailed one hundred miles to the north of any trace of civilization, my crew and I found ourselves and our ship hemmed in by mountains and endless plains of ice. In this desolate predicament, about two o'clock one afternoon, we saw to our astonishment a dog-sled racing north, and bearing upon it a being of truly gigantic stature.

A few hours later, to our vast relief, the ice broke, but the twilight was much too far advanced to set sail till morning. On the morrow, my crew discovered on a sledge near the side of the ship a second man, much smaller in stature. He had but one dog remaining. It was immediately apparent that his health was gravely compromised and we persuaded him to come on board.

As he languished by the galley stove, he unfolded in halting English a truly frightening history. His name was Victor Frankenstein, by birth a Genevese, his family one of the most distinguished of that republic.

You may recall how, in an earlier letter, I lamented that amongst my crew I have no friend capable of the kind of communication I have sorely missed: a man possessed of a cultivated and capacious mind, to approve or amend my plans. I was sure that I should find no such friend on the wide ocean; yet in Victor Frankenstein I have found a man who, before his spirit had been broken by misery, I should have been happy to have possessed as the brother of my heart, for when he speaks, though his words are culled with the choicest art, they flow with rapidity and unparallelled eloquence.

I, who have spent six long years learning navigation and earning funds to purchase a ship, hire a crew and set sail to discover the mysteries of the North Pole, discovered in Victor Frankenstein an ambition as singular as mine own; nay, more so, for he was a student of natural philosophy, and devoted himself to testing the boundaries between life and death.

With a surgeon's skill, Victor Frankenstein put together limbs and other parts of corpses (forgive me, Sister, for this necessary gruesomeness). Infusing his creation with electricity drawn from the skies, he brought his creature to life—only to reel away from it, horrified, for it was a hideous thing!

I should write that it *is* a hideous thing, for it was he whom my crew spied, that giant on the first sled. Frankenstein was literally pursuing him to the ends of the earth. He meant to revenge himself on the creature for murdering his bride, his closest friend Henry Clerval, and his younger brother William, whose death was blamed on an innocent girl named Justine Moritz, who was hanged for it. Frankenstein also charged his foe with the death of his father from grief.

I met the fearsome creature on the night that Frankenstein died.

It had been a bleak day. My crew had been threatening mutiny, and at length they exacted my promise that as soon as the ice cleared (for we were caught in it again), I would turn the ship toward home. On the afternoon of September 19th, cracks and rumblings resounded at a distance, and for a time we feared the vessel would be ground between the jagged teeth of the breaking floe, but as the water-way opened, a breeze sprang up and our passage to safety seemed assured.

This meant the end of my ambitious drive north and put an end as well to my guest Frankenstein's quest for revenge.

"Do you then really return?" he asked me.

"Alas! yes; I cannot withstand my crew's demands. My conscience will not permit me to lead them unwillingly into new dangers, and therefore I must return to England."

"Do so, if you will; but I will not," Frankenstein declared. "You may give up your purpose, but mine is assigned to me by heaven, and I dare not abandon it. I am weak; but surely the spirits who assist my vengeance will endow me with sufficient strength." Saying this, he endeavoured to spring from the bed, but the exertion was too great for him, and he fell back upon the mattress, and fainted.

What little remaining strength he had possessed was altogether dissipated and soon he told me that he knew he was about to die. Our doctor administered to him a composing draught, but whispered to me that the patient had scant hours left of life.

I stayed by his bed-side. When he woke, Frankenstein uttered his last thoughts about the strange creation he had brought about—sentiments that his creature also heard, as I later discovered.

"During these last days," said Frankenstein, "I have been occupied in examining my past conduct. In a fit of enthusiastic madness I created a rational creature, and was bound towards him, to assure, as far as was in my power, his happiness and well-being. This, however, I failed in and the mistake shattered my life. He displayed unparalleled malignity and a nature made evil by mine own error, and for my neglect, nay, utter repudation of he who I had brought to life, this miserably unhappy creature destroyed my friends; indeed, he devoted to destruction superior beings who possessed exquisite sensation, happiness, and wisdom; nor do I know where this thirst for vengeance may end. That he may render none other wretched, he ought to die, but not altogether in the spirit of revenge, for his brooding existence brings him naught but pain. The task of his destruction was mine, but I have failed. Farewell, Walton! Seek happiness in tranquility, and avoid ambition, even if it be the apparently innocent one of distinguishing yourself in science and discoveries."

Soon afterward, he died. I went to my cabin to write a letter to you whilst his last words were still fresh in my memory. As I was thus engaged, along about midnight, I heard a hoarse voice coming from the place where Frankenstein's relict lay. I went there to investigate and was shocked to see standing over the corpse of his maker that giant I had heard of in such hideous detail.

His size was awesome; huge, yet misshapen; his hair was ragged; his complexion as colourless as a mummy's windings. It was all that I could do not to swoon at the dreadful sight, yet he uttered such exclamations of grief and horror that in spite of my loathing, I could not help but pity this wholly wretched creature.

Suddenly he saw me and made to spring for the window and escape, but I called upon him to stay. He looked on me with such wonder that, in spite of my fear, aversion and anger, my heart yet was touched.

"That is also my victim!" he exclaimed. "In his death my crimes are consummated. Oh, Frankenstein! Generous and self-devoted being! What does it avail that I now ask you to pardon me? I, who irretrievably destroyed all those whom you loved. Alas! he is cold; he may not answer me."

"Your repentance is superfluous," I told him. "If you had but listened to the voice of conscience, and heeded the stings of remorse before you had urged your diabolical vengeance to this extremity, Frankenstein would yet have lived."

"And do you imagine that I was then dead to agony and remorse?" he cried, wringing his hands and, I confess, mine own heart. "A frightful selfishness hurried me on, wherefore all the while my spirit was aching with remorse. Think ye that the groans of Henry Clerval or those of Elizabeth, Frankenstein's dying bride, were music to my ears? My heart was fashioned to be susceptible to love and sympathy; but, when wrenched by misery to vice and hatred, it did not endure the violence of the change without torture."

O, Sister, when I was a student, I read in translation from the Greek a composition, *Gorgias*, an unusually impassioned Platonic dialogue in which Socrates maintains that one who does sinful things is more miserable than those who suffer the results of those same evil actions. Now in my youth, I did not accept the truth of that idea, but now I do, for never was there a better example of that Socratic opinion than the anguish of Frankenstein's unnatural creation.

I was torn between compassion and righteous rage. "Wretch!" said I, "it is well that you come here to whine over the desolation you have made. You throw a torch into a pile of buildings, and when they are consumed, you sit among the ruins, and lament the structure's fall. It is not pity that you feel; you lament only because the victim of your malignity is at last withdrawn from your power."

"Oh, it is not thus," the being interrupted me. "But in all fairness, what other impression can you possibly have? I do not expect, nor deserve your sympathy. Virtue has become to me a shadow of a value beyond my comprehension, and therefore I must suffer. You who befriended poor Victor Frankenstein seem to have knowledge of his misfortunes and my crimes, but let me reassure you that you need not fear that I shall be the instrument of future mischief. I shall perform only one further act of violence, and that will be upon myself. I confess to having a desire to travel to the North Pole, and when I reach that place—"

(Here, he unwittingly voiced my own ambition!)

"O, do not think I mean to arrive there upon this vessel," he continued, "for I shall quit your ship, and will seek the globe's northern extremity by mine own labours. When I get there, I shall build from my ice-raft and whatever detritus I can take away with me, a funeral pyre, and consume to ashes this miserable, misshapen frame of mine. I shall die so that I may cease to feel the agonies which now consume me. Light, feeling, and sense, will pass away. Torn by the bitterest remorse, where can I find rest but in death?"

With that, he vaulted onto his ice-raft, and I watched him borne away upon the waves, until he was lost in darkness and distance.

*

My dear Margaret, to comprehend the events that happened shortly afterward you must know something of the character of my crew, and that will soon be manifest to you. In an earlier letter, I told you about two of them. The ship's master was a gentle soul who, having sacrificed his life's happiness for the woman he loved, was, I fear, glad to be the first to succumb to the rigours of the frozen north.

The other, my English lieutenant, was a noble savage riddled with national and professional prejudices un-tempered by cultivation, yet he possessed great stamina and courage. His virtue and his flaw was that he was madly desirous of glory. Thus he was furious at the crew for prevailing upon me to turn the ship towards home. More than once, he impugned them all to their faces as craven foreigners (though he said something rather worse than "foreigners").

We buried Victor Frankenstein the next morning. Ceremonies were necessarily brief, for my crew was anxious to set sail. I muttered a few words at my friend's grave, which was nothing more than a hacked-out trench in the tundra, and then with a nod to my lieutenant to assume command, I crossed the gang-way and shut myself up in my cabin.

To take so passive a role at that critical juncture in our failed venture now strikes me as negligent. Yet in my defense I cite the toll of the tiring vigil spent for days at the bed-side of my dying friend, a watch that made me labour diligently to preserve a written record of his tragic life, the difficulty of which you may surmise from its great length and detail. Also in my defence, the preceding day and night were rife with incident: Victor Frankenstein's passing and that strange midnight interview with his nameless creation. I had slept but little, and what rest I had was troubled. And yet still my conscience taxes me, for this temporary abrogation of responsibility directly led to the spilling of blood. But innocent of the danger, I shut the door, collapsed upon my bunk and, exhausted and depressed, fell fast asleep until the morrow morn.

*

Shouts and angry voices woke me up. Before my eyes could open of their own accord, my cabin door was flung wide and rough hands seized me.

"What is the meaning of this outrage?" I demanded, struggling to sit up. My arms were pinioned by the ship's carpenter. His mate grabbed my legs. Together, they lugged me onto the deck like a potato sack and dumped me by the ship's wheel.

The helm was unmanned. I grasped it and steadied the vessel, which had been turning in a slow arc through the icy sea. As I returned my attention top-side, it struck me that my lieutenant was nowhere to be seen.

I heard a noise. Looking aft from whence the sound proceeded, I was horrified to see our cook sprawled against a mast, clutching his side. Blood streamed over his fingers.

I demanded to know what the reason was for this atrocity.

"We took control of the helm," said the carpenter. "That's when Lieutenant gored him with his knife."

"He obviously regarded your action as mutiny. Why would you seize the wheel? None of you are expert steersmen."

"Because you betrayed us, Captain."

"Betrayed you?" I echoed. "How?"

"He was taking us *further north!*"

The truth smote me like a fist, and I protested that he had taken action on his own, not my authority, but the crew would not believe in my innocence.

The carpenter's mate called all hands on deck, which meant but seven remaining men, plus the doctor. He busied himself with the cook's wounds, but the set of his jaw showed that he held little hope that the man would survive.

"Where is the lieutenant?" I asked. By way of reply, the carpenter jabbed his fore-finger over the side of the vessel and down.

He polled the crew and my fate was sealed: I was to follow the lieutenant. In vain I protested. I argued that without my sailing knowledge, they risked wrecking the vessel. The doctor tried to speak for me, but the carpenter, drunk with power (and assuredly with rum), so therefore heedless to the danger, pitched him into the sea.

The crew, upset by this rash, unthinking act of violence, insisted that I be shown mercy (if a choice between slow or swift death can be viewed as merciful), so I was not drowned, but set, instead, upon the tundra. I was given a small amount of food, a canteen, and the papers in my cabin, including this letter, though I doubted that it would ever reach you. And thus fortune's reversal—for less than an hour before, I had been asleep in my cabin, and now I stood upon a vast shelf of hard-packed snow watching my stolen vessel make its way south.

We had already sailed far north of the last outposts of civilization, and I despaired of another vessel ever rescuing me. I knew that it was not within my power to hike southward for more than a hundred Arctic miles, even if the intervening land were a solid mass, which it is not. My choice appeared to be to stay where I was, eventually to die, or to turn further north and perish trying to attain my original goal and set eyes upon the North Pole. You may imagine, Sister, what I elected to do.

A weary time now passed; I trudged and trudged north-ward, and though I wore a pair of dark glasses, my eyes were still dazzled by the landscape's unrelieved white glare. I rested standing, for I feared that if I lay down, I would not rise again. How long I stumbled along I cannot tell; time and the glaring snow-drifts melded together, and my thoughts flowed as sluggishly as my blood.

At length, I have no idea how long it was, my limbs grew so stiff with cold, and my feet became so leaden that I could not take another step. I sank to my knees and fumbled at my food store, but my jaws lacked the strength to take even a bite of hard tack. Even sighing seemed an effort as I slumped onto my side and waited for sleep and death to close my crusted eye-lids.

When the light altered, I studied it incuriously for what might have been minutes or hours. At length, though it cost my numb mind ponderous effort, I came to realize that what I beheld, and now heard close by, was a great bonfire. With my last bit of strength I uttered a feeble cry.

A surprised gasp, a brief silence save for the crackling flames, and then I heard the loud crunch of approaching footsteps. Strong arms lifted me, and my canteen was tipped to my lips. I swallowed a mouthful of brandy and then my mind descended into darkness.

When I woke again, I lay by the fire. My limbs had thawed and felt cramped and painful, but I was alive. I tried to sit up. A huge hand pressed me back down.

"Rest," a harsh voice commanded. "Soon I will feed you."

Recognizing the voice that I had heard at midnight, I gazed up into watery eyes that were near the same hue as the dun white sockets Victor Frankenstein had set them in.

"You who killed so many, why have you saved my life?"

The creature's lips curled in a smile ghastly to behold. "Even a wretch may believe in the workings of Providence. I built my funeral pile, and meant to welcome its torrid embrace, when here at the North Pole where I never expected to meet another living being, I heard your cry."

"This cannot be the Pole," I protested, "it is further north."

He shook his head and showed me his compass. Its needle dipped downward.

I stared, mystified, at the phenomenon, and only later recollected that in my studies I had read of the discoveries of the navigator deCastro and of William Gilbert, who claimed the earth itself is a great magnet, its hub of attraction not quite congruent with the geographical Pole.

I grant you that my original intent was to visit the true North Pole, yet here, accidentally collaborating with Victor Frankenstein, I had satisfied my ambition and stripped away one of earth's mysteries, proving that William Gilbert's theory must be correct.

Dear Sister, I realized this only upon reflection, for when the giant held out his compass, I confess I denied the evidence that it showed to me almost as vehemently as I refused to accept that my friend's foe had saved my life.

"Captain Walton," he said with surprising mildness, "you are my creator's last living friend, yet when you first set thine eyes upon me, you did not drive me off. And though you taxed me with those crimes for which my maker himself could not loathe me half so much as I myself, yet in your eyes I also thought I saw compassion."

I admitted freely that I pitied him, at least for that early time when his spirit was still capable of love.

"That is why I mean to bring you home safe. Now close your eyes and sleep."

He kept his promise. Nursing me, nourishing me, keeping me warm, he made a litter of his sled and pulled me behind as he walked tirelessly south. I marveled at his strength and endurance. The cold did not affect him as it did me.

After more than a week of slow journeying (he seldom slept, and not for long), we came upon my ship, once more trapped in the ice. By now, I was sufficiently recovered to walk without his aid. As I had feared, the mutineers were incapable of sailing her safely home-ward.

Frankenstein's creature was reluctant to show himself to the sailors, but lest I be offered harm, he accompanied me on board. But of the seven remaining crew members, six were not in sight, and only the carpenter's mate still lived, though not for long. We found him in his cabin, wounded and burning up with fever.

Amazed at my return, he roused what little strength he had left and told me what had occurred after I was marooned. "It was the carpenter," he gasped. "He decided that there was neither food enough nor rum for us all, so he slashed their throats while they slept and threw them over the side. But then he turned on me." He began to laugh, but the ghastly noise declined to a cough. "Not before I did 'im proper."

It was at this fell moment that the giant made his appearance. Neither he nor I were prepared for the effect that this had upon the carpenter's mate. Sick as he was, when he saw that great misshapen figure looming in the door's entry, the sick man sprang up with a cry that was part exclamation, part scream, and all horror. Till then I did not know that he still clutched the blade he had used to defend himself against the carpenter. Before that danger could register, the carpenter's mate (I think his name was Lawrence) ripped a great slash across the creature's mid-riff. The monster (Dear Sister, what else may I call him?) cried out in pain, and then, with a demonic howl, he approached his attacker...but then—I am still astonished to recall this!—the creature's eyes caught mine, and with an effort that must have cost him every ounce of restraint which his history reveals he does not and never has possessed, he actually backed away, only one step, but for him it might have been a mile. The carpenter's mate again raised his knife and was about to stab the giant once more when, without thinking, I cried out, "For God's sake! Defend yourself!"

With that encouragement, the creature smashed his great fist against his attacker's throat. It was only one blow, but it was more than sufficient; it wholly finished the man. I reminded myself that his life was already a window away from being shut forever, and yet the horrific power of that killing blow was so dreadfully intense that my senses quitted me and I fell to the deck in a swoon.

*

Once I roused, the creature told me that he had found what was left of the carpenter in the galley. We gave his and his mate's bodies up to the sea. When all was done, the creature submitted to my dressing of his wound as best I could, considering my scant medical knowledge and the dearth of hospital supplies.

He murmured something that I thought I had perhaps misheard. Therefore, I asked him to repeat it.

"Violence," he said, "is sickening."

*

My beloved Margaret, to pilot a vessel of any size with only two able hands would be altogether impossible, but this creature's astonishing strength and fortitude, even considering his injuries, has made an impossibility merely a very difficult thing. When the ice at length broke and we reached the first frontier post of civilization, he entreated me not to take on a crew.

"If you do," he explained, "I must needs confine myself below for the rest of the voyage, and the chance of one of the men discovering me might prove disastrous, as you may well imagine."

Indeed, I did imagine it and shuddered at the thought, and so I reluctantly agreed to accept his plan. The notion of crossing the seas with him alone is more unsettling than I may have been able to convey to you, for dear Margaret, if I have not made this altogether clear by now, do understand, then, that he is mind-numbingly horrifying to behold! Though, to be fair—fairer, perhaps, than any has ever offered him, till now—he speaks to me as gently as his harsh voice allows him to, and while he has never made any gesture to me that might be construed to be in the least bit threatening, his bloody history still plays havoc with my imagination.

Well, at his request (I would not think of saying no!), our ultimate destination has, at last, been determined—it is the Orkney isles just north of Scotland, a place that he says he once journeyed to. Actually, it is a rather good choice, for the Orkneys constitute the closest land-fall that we might hope to reach.

The injury which he sustained refuses to heal. I told him that on the mainland of Scotland, I know a man whose medical skill might perhaps help him. Professor Abel MacMorris is now retired and lives some fifty miles above Edinburgh in Pitlochry, a village just south of, and sometimes called the gateway to, the Highlands.

The poor giant—yes, Dear Margaret, I have begun to think of him as a soul in need of, and perhaps even deserving of, rescue! He must needs now travel south but without my company, for I must linger at least until I can sell my ship at whatever profit I might be able to realize.

I told him that if and when it is possible, I would join him and Professor Abel MacMorris in the regions somewhere close to Pitlochry. The creature told me that he has decided not to immolate himself, as he had originally intended, but hopes, instead, to settle somewhere in the Scottish country-side, possibly living as a hermit. He swears to me that he will never again harm any living soul.

I pray, Sister, that he keeps his word!

I have given this letter to a Norwegian sea captain whom I have met in port. He promises to pass it on to the first English vessel that he may encounter.

Your affectionate brother,

Robert Walton

PART ONE

In Pitlochry Forest

1 TAKE A NAME

All Things Without a Name Are Evil.

In my early days, when I was innocent and hungry for knowledge, I secretly listened to books being read to a blind man, and that is when I first heard this harsh sentiment penned by an obscure French philosopher—*All Things Without a Name Are Evil*.

It made me feel utterly miserable. Everything I could call to mind had names: Victor, Ernest, William, Henry, Elizabeth, Justine; juices, meats, even lakes, mountains, trees, wild flowers; bears, eagles, wolves. None were wicked like me, for savage beasts are fashioned by Nature for their own survival. But my creator did not deign to name me, and the only words that people ever hurl at me like stones are curses, though they have thrown stones, as well. They have all treated me as their enemy because I am ugly, huge, and, I admit it, quite misshapen. They have persecuted me with fire-arms, torches, and bludgeons. Most of them, I am sure, have never felt the snap of neck-bones, or heard the death-rattle, yet they are monsters like me, though when they kill, as I have perceived it, it is generally in the name of their gods.

The acts that ended my innocence have been told elsewhere. I meant to die as an ultimate penance, but since that decision, I have come to appreciate that the harder, necessary choice for me is to live. Necessary it is because, although I have told Captain Walton that I would become a hermit and do no futher injury, that does not seem to me to be anything even close to approximating what I must do. No, with reflection, I have decided that I must try to devote the rest of my life to ever so many acts of contrition, and perhaps more than that, **sacrifice**! Although how that might be brought about, I am in no way sure—but I do hope, somehow, that—however unlikely—I may at last manage to expunge these black marks that I myself have burned upon my soul.

And yet—do I have a *soul*?

They say that mermaids, elves and leprechauns have no such thing, but these mythic folk at least have the companionship of their own kind, whereas I am ever alone. But if I *do* possess this soul-thing that none ever can see nor describe, my deeds have certainly soiled its pristine state with blood, so then, in spite of my wish to do penance, I do not think that I can perform any action at all to wash this impenetrable entity, if it exists at all—clean...can I? (Yes, of course, Father Naman takes considerable issue with this view and has ever and again counseled me to do good deeds, no matter whether those actions be great or small).

And yet ...

All things without a name are evil.

That, at least, I may remedy. For if I choose a name for myself, perhaps something like a soul will take root and anchor me to that life of penitence which I hope and mean to pursue.

But still—what name should I choose? Some fathers do call their sons after themselves. May not a son, then, do the same thing?

Therefore I shall write it boldly—

FRANKENSTEIN

In this perhaps hubristic act of taking to myself my father's name (my creator being the closest approximation I have to a conventional progenitor), I feel both newly connected with my past, yet also broken free of it. Writing it boldly, I do not imagine that any eyes but mine will ever read it. And yet I have determined to commit my story to paper, and if any of Frankenstein's race ever come upon it, I do not suppose that they will show me mercy, for soon or late, they will track me down, and though I am swift, strong and cunning, even I am no match for gun-fire.

Still, if I do set forth the facts as accurately as I am able, who knows but that some insight will transpire, and I might actually be able to understand myself.

Thus, what follows is my latter history.

Of some happenings, I lacked direct knowledge, so, when possible, I questioned those persons who were somehow involved and set forth their witness as near as memory permits. In other instances, when direct witness was not possible, I have tried to inscribe that which what must most likely have happened—though, perhaps, in those passages I have indulged myself ultimately in fantasy, yet I do hope that I have done so with scrupulous fairness. Thus, such portions of my story, whether they are direct reportage or devised as honestly as I could, by me, are each prefaced by each narrator's name in parentheses.

You who read my words may disbelieve what I am about to tell you, but I was not born. A Genevese student of natural philosophy named Victor Frankenstein fashioned me from cadavers and employed both chemistry and electricity to infuse me with life. He is dead now, though I did not kill him—at least not directly.

When first I woke, my maker regarded me with such abhorrence that he utterly abandoned me. Confused and lonely, I took garments from his wardrobe and wandered through the adjoining Swiss forest until I encountered a family who lived there.

Secretly I watched them and listened as they spoke, day after day, and as they taught English to one of their guests I learned how to read and write. I did chores for these folk, whom I came to love.

Naturally they were mystified that they had an unseen benefactor, but were pleased at this seemingly capricious source of aid. At length I ventured to introduce myself to the eldest of their circle. Because he was blind, I felt he would not shun me, and indeed, he welcomed me kindly enough, but when his kinfolk caught me with him, they, horrified at my appearance and great ungainly size, beat me with a stick till I fled.

Their unthinking cruelty broke my heart, yet because I loved them still, toward them I harboured no bitterness.

But another event had a markedly different effect upon me. One day as I passed a clearing in the woods, I saw a young woman playing along the edge of a swift stream. Her foot slipped and she fell in, screaming. I leapt into the flood and rescued her, but no sooner had I brought her back to shore when a youth darted out of the forest, snatched her from my arms, and shot me. Though I had saved a human being's life, my rewards for my selfless action were suffering and pain.

It was then that I vowed eternal vengeance against the race of men.

Old memories arise and I grow angry, but this is not good. I made a promise to Captain Walton and to myself, and I will do my best to honour it. Yet it is hard to repress the rage I have long felt at the injustice mankind has visited upon me again and again.

After I rescued and helped bring Captain Walton to safety, I yearned to return to Switzerland, for the Alpine forest always brought solace to my spirit. But I knew its spell now was broken, for my homeland holds too many painful memories. I considered settling, instead, in Scotland, for when my creator passed through England and its northern neighbour, journeying to the Orkneys to create a bride for me, I trailed him, step by step, keeping to the woods and skirting the edges of towns; I travel swift and need little sleep, so I easily kept pace with him.

Once I set foot in the territory the Scots call The Borders, I was awe-struck with its majesty. Imagine a great rolling landscape whose abundance produces new wonders every few miles: tawny grass-land dotted with great round bales of hay, stallions galloping for sheer pleasure, mountains smaller than the Alps, yet more ominous and brooding, sparkling rivers where salmon spawn and leap. If ever my sins are quit and I am permitted to enter Paradise, I think it shall resemble Scotland.

Once the captain's ship neared a navigable landing, the memory of my last visit overwhelmed me. Frankenstein feared that the woman he was making for me would, together with myself, produce a race of monsters, inimical to mankind. He was mistaken, not knowing of the limitations that effectively hedged the life which he had promiscuously spawned in my misshapen body, for, though he apparently did not realize this fact, even the preliminaries of the act are, for me, profoundly frustrating. It is not within my power to procreate.

O Frankenstein, I sought the solace of her companionship, nothing more!

Well, I peered each and every night through the window of the laboratory he had built for the supposed purpose of providing me a mate. I watched as my intended companion was slowly assembled, piece by piece.

I suppose that she was hideous, but, of course, by any human standard, so am I. And therefore, waiting for Victor Frankenstein to invest this distaff entity with life, I was visited in slumber by a recurring nightmare that she would open her eyes, see me, and reject me in horror and disgust. To counter my fears, I tried to imagine myself comforting her after she came upon that homeliest of diabolic instruments … a mirror.

But as I waited for her to live, I grew more fearful of that moment when she would draw breath for the first time. What if she cursed me when she learned that I had caused her to be created? And yet, as I contemplated the future, the pleasanter I found her to look upon, for the face is not the index of the spirit, and love's rough chemistry had begun to stir within my breast.

So when Frankenstein suddenly slashed her to pieces, and she who had never lived yet died, so did every last vestige of my hope.

I *must* keep to the point—the injury which I sustained upon Captain Walton's ship refuses to heal, and so my very first business must be to find the physician whom the Captain recommended.

Once Walton and I parted, I sought out caves and uninhabited shacks, avoiding villages and towns, and worked my way through the Highlands till the rugged terrain grew less wild. One morning I came upon a peaceful river valley, which I learned is a short walk from Pitlochry, near where Captain Walton said Professor MacMorris lives. I was not sure how to trace him, so I found a cave and dwelt therein as I puzzled over my prospects.

Each morning, I would make my way to the edge of the woods and gaze across a heathery meadow to houses and small farms in the distance, but I lacked the courage to draw near. I returned to this spot day after day, trying to think of a plan. One morning, footsteps behind me surprised and startled me. I whirled and saw a young red-haired girl with a basket on her arm gazing in my direction. She seemed to stare at me head-on, but I saw no fear, nor any expression other than perplexity, and that is when I realized that she must be blind.

"Is someone there?" she called. She waited for an answer, but, receiving none, tossed her curls impatiently. "If that's you, Robbie

Pratt, do not think to frighten me, for I can take you on straight enough, with or without my father. And keep your hands to yourself or it will be injury that you're courting, and not Eve MacMorris!" With that she strode briskly out of the forest, across the lea, and into town.

This feisty girl delighted me. Being blind, she would not spurn to be my friend, I thought, yet she had mentioned her father, and though that bespoke caution, I wondered if he might be the very man whom I had been seeking?

I waited till she came back, and perhaps an hour later she returned. Aware that those without vision often have acute hearing, I kept some distance off, yet managed to follow her to a glade half the distance between my cave and town. In it stood a modest log cabin with a porch and a few glass windows in its walls.

As she approached her home, the door opened and a stocky, middle-aged man with copper hair like his daughter greeted her. They hugged and went inside.

Walking softly, I rested against one of the cabin walls and listened through an open window as Eve prepared their meal.

I became their constant eavesdropper. By the time a few days had elapsed, I pieced together the facts. He was, indeed, Professor Abel MacMorris, a former Edinburgh teacher and scientist who resigned when his eyes began growing what Shakespeare calls "sand-blind." I mean his vision is limited; he discerns light, shadow and shape, but none of them are well-defined. I doubted that he could help me, after all.

Eve is perhaps fifteen years old and has been blind since birth, a defect the Professor blamed on her mother, who lives in Scotland's capital, Edinburgh, where the Professor once worked. With her long, strong countenance bracketed by twin falls of orange curly hair, Eve is no fairy-child; she has a mouth and a mind, and is not afraid to use them. Her father encourages her to do so, for before he retired, his was a life of thought and so he respects her capacity to express hers.

It was selfish of me to feel glad that neither of them could truly see me, yet here was a family, complete unto itself, that might accept the good will I bore them. But I held back from meeting them. I was all too aware of the similarity between the Professor and the blind man in the Swiss woods who befriended me before his kin-folk drove me off. I feared a repetition of that incident, even though the parallel here seemed favourably altered by Eve's sightlessness.

For many days, I surreptitiously observed them. They appeared to have no friends or relatives other than themselves, but seemed content in that circumstance, and that worked to my advantage. Their sole visitor was the lad Robbie Pratt, a lanky youth of sixteen who was clearly attracted to Eve. I thought that I had better avoid him.

I wondered what provender the MacMorris family lived on. Twice I followed Eve's trips into town. Stopping at the last trees, I would wait till she returned, laden with simple fare bought or begged, I had no idea.

I began to do little things for them. I cleared debris from their porch and cleansed the windows so light would better penetrate the cabin, thus benefiting his failing vision. These things they would not be likely to notice, but then I perceived that Abel's most difficult chore was securing fire-wood, a task beyond Eve's capacity, though she was wonderfully adept in cleaning the cabin, lighting the stove and cooking their meals.

That night, borrowing Abel's hatchet and going off a goodly distance so the chopping would not disturb their slumbers, I cut them fire-wood, and repeated this every other night, never enough, I thought, so that they would notice that the pile was not diminishing as swiftly as before. But in this, I was mistaken. They soon became aware of my labour, though I did not yet know what tell-tale had given me away.

MacMorris thought Robbie Pratt was trying to impress them, but Eve dismissed the notion.

"Robbie doing any sort of hard labour? Father, you are *so* wrong!" she proclaimed with a laugh. "I think we have a guardian angel watching over us!"

"My dear daughter, you cannot be serious!"

"Father," Eve laughed, "I don't mean some cherub or seraph complete with wings and halo! But whoever has been helping us surely is a function of the essential goodness of Fate."

Nevertheless, MacMorris began to look troubled and, though she protested, he began insisting on accompanying her on her trips into town, though walking wearied him.

That is when I knew that I must declare myself. I did not want to cause stress to this good man, so, not without internal struggle, I resolved that I would risk speaking to him.

One bright May morning Eve cleared away the breakfast dishes and said she wished to swim. Her father tried to talk her out of it, but she scoffed at his fears, so the two of them set out through the woods and soon came upon a cool forest glade. A brook rippling through it dropped some fifteen or sixteen feet into a deep pond. This is where Eve chose to splash and play, partly hidden by the waterfall's descending curtain.

Her father rested on a tree-stump, and turned up his face to feel the dappled light breaking through the dewy leaves and branches. I admired his red hair with its ruffled grey wings, his round apple-cheeks and his smile of uncommon sweetness.

I took a step toward him. Sensing my presence, he addressed me amiably. "I think 'tis you who has been chopping fire-wood for us. If you mean us no harm, come and take my hand and call me friend."

I stumbled closer. He turned toward the blot my body made in the sunlight.

"Och, now, they fashioned you on a grand scale!"

Truer than he realized. Fearing the harshness of my voice, I replied softly, "I am that which people call a giant."

"Aye, but a gentle giant, I think. Sit by me, friend…why, what is wrong?" His eye-sight was dim, but his ears were acute, and he heard me crying.

"You are kind to me. I am unaccustomed to that." I wanted to rest my head on his shoulder, but such emotion might disconcert him; he was, after all, a Scot.

Regaining self-control, I sat down by his side and, taking care not to squeeze it, grasped his hand. "How did you know that I chopped your wood? I did it far from the cabin."

He smiled. "A man with diminished vision pays special attention to what he is still able to see." He waited to learn whether I took his meaning, and I did.

"I did not put the axe back in its customary place!"

"Precisely," he replied, "but that mystery was easily solved. What I do not understand is why you took a stranger's labours upon yourself. Though perhaps that is not such a puzzle, after all."

"Why?"

"Because when I showed you common courtesy just now, you wept." He brushed his fingers over the palms of my hands. "The roughness of your skin bespeaks a hard life, one without friendship. Laddie, you are a man who has endured great pain, have you not?"

He pitied me. Yet if he possessed better sight, he would surely shrink away, and if he knew the nature of my crimes, his generous heart surely would harden.

"I *have* known pain," I admitted, "but I have also caused much suffering."

"I take you at your word, but I sense no danger in you now. Whatever you have done, are you not now deeply sorry for it?"

"How can you know?! I am a stranger whom you see but dimly!"

MacMorris patted my hand. "There are two kinds of knowledge, that of the mind, and that of the heart. These are things a scientist might scoff at, but if you've lived long enough, you sense some things without the benefit of the five senses. Among such phenomena is the spirit, and yours, I believe, is that of a penitent."

This good, gentle man accorded me a spirit of mine own!

His next question, though, troubled me. "I am, or, rather, was Professor MacMorris, Abel Harrison MacMorris. What is your name, friend?"

I had only chosen a single name, but he had *three*! It struck me that if I declared my name to be Frankenstein, it might not be unknown to him. He may have heard about the charge of murder my maker was subjected to after I destroyed his friend Henry Clerval, for though it had happened in Ireland, the news may well have reached Scottish eyes and ears.

When one tells a lie, Fate must jot it down for future punishment.

"What is your name?" he asked, and the only one that came to mind was that of the young man who fancied Eve, Robbie Pratt. I decided to pretend it was mine, too. But what first name should I take? Names of two of my victims came to mind; I almost answered "William Henry Pratt," but feared it would be too much for me to remember, so instead I just said, "Willie Pratt."

"Be you a relative of young Robbie's?"

One lie begets another. "We're distant cousins, though we have never met."

"Really?" (*Was he doubtful?*) "What brings you to this out-o'-the way spot?"

"Someone told me that you might be able to help me—"

Our conversation was suddenly cut short. A shrill cry rang out. MacMorris leapt to his feet.

"It's *Eve!*"

A BIZARRE DISCOVERY

(Professor MacMorris)

Eve's scream and my new friend's harsh cry were coupled with high laughter from that rascal Robbie Pratt, but when the giant leapt up (shifting shadows and shuffling sounds told me that he did so), the lad's mirth changed to a terrified yell, followed by an enormous splash. Though some distance from the water, yet I was doused. Scrambling to my feet, I shouted, "What's happening? Eve, are you all right?"

"Yes!" she called.

"Where are you?"

"Behind the falls. Robbie snatched my clothes!"

"Where's Willie?"

"Who?"

"Willie?" Robbie echoed. "Is that what that thing calls itself?"

"*What* thing?" Eve demanded.

"The chap who has been chopping our wood. Where is he?!"

"He jumped in," said Robbie. "Hasn't come up yet."

"Ninny!" Eve exclaimed, "there's edges and rocks! *Help him!*"

The next moments, for me, consisted of cobwebs, slants and shafts—I mean, those dappled patterns of light my failing eyes perceived. There was a confused mélange of sound—splashes, grunts, panting, mild imprecations (Robbie, o' course), and then I heard loud choking noises coming from somewhere in the water.

This, I soon learned, is what had happened—when the giant leapt in to save Eve from non-existent dangers, he hit his head against a rock and lost consciousness. It was all Robbie could do to haul him to the surface. He proved too heavy for him, so Robbie struggled to keep their heads above water till at last, "Will...Willie" (I suspect that's not his name) managed to drag himself onto the bank, where I heard him gasping, coughing and groaning.

I knelt by his side. "Where does it hurt, Will?"

"My leg."

"May I palpate? I will be gentle."

He guided my hand; I focused my attention, then removed my fingers. "I think that it is broken. Can you stand?"

An indrawn hiss. He tried to, but could not manage it.

"Robbie," I said, "guide me home, I must fashion a splint." I patted the victim's arm. "Rest. I will be back soon. Eve will stay with you." I grasped Robbie's arm and we set off along the trail. When we'd walked far enough to be out of ear-shot, the boy cleared his throat. "Professor, how can y' leave Eve alone with him?" Using my title told me that Robbie was troubled; his usual cocky habit is to call me "Mister Mac."

"He hurt himself trying to *rescue* her!"

"But he's a stranger!"

"He says that he is your distant cousin."

"Rubbish! I know every man, bairn and grown, in my clan!"

"Maybe there is a branch that ye're not aware of?"

"If there was, do you think that any Pratt would look like *that*? Begging your pardon, Professor, but you canna see him all that clearly!"

"Robbie, he is very big, that I know."

"*Big?* I'm big...he's a *monster!*"

"Come, lad, that is unkind. I can tell from his shadow, he is uneven ... lop-sided?"

Robbie halted. "It is more than a matter of size or how he walks."

"All right, lad. Describe him."

"He's—*It's* all out o' kilter! His hair's a mess, his skin is so pale y'd think he did not ha' a drop o' blood in him, though, to be fair, there's a red gash 'crost his belly."

"A man should not be measured solely by physical comeliness."

"But I haven't told y' the strangest thing..."

What Robbie said next seemed far too strange to believe.

But as we returned to the pond and I braced the victim's leg, I palpated and perceived that what Robbie had told me was true, and it was truly bizarre.

"Will" understood what I was doing, and what I had discovered.

"Yes, Professor," he said, "my hands and limbs and feet were sewn on."

A long silence. I decided not to badger him with my questions while he was in pain. He knew that I would want to know more, so I trusted that he would explain when he was ready, and not a moment before.

I helped him to his feet.

OF PAIN, FRIENDSHIP
NIGHTMARE

While I waited for the Professor to return with the fixings of a splint, I lay upon the grass, groaning. Not only did my left leg pain me, the slash of the sailor's knife across my middle gaped wider. Eve asked me if there were anything she might do to help. I could think of nothing, but she took it on herself to hold my head in her lap and sing. I cried in earnest then, partly because of her kindness, but more so because I feared what Robbie must be telling her father about me on their way to the cabin. I had not reckoned, though, on my new friend's goodness. Now I would never minimize Captain Walton's role in helping me in my attempt to tame my tormented spirit, but Walton's compassion is coupled with a bed-rock revulsion that he can not succeed in hiding from me, and it reflects all too accurately mine own self-loathing.

But when Professor MacMorris returned and, during his ministrations, discovered those scars where Frankenstein had sewn me together, I hinted of my laboratory origins. He, although consumed, I am sure, by curiosity and foreboding, brushed aside his doubts and questions and, helping me up, propped a large branch under my arm so that I could rest my weight against it, and rebandaged my wound.

This act of kindness worked in me a powerful emotion, virtually an epiphany, though at that moment I neither knew that word nor the concept behind it. Father Naman later defined it for me, and I came to realize that what I had experienced then was not a religious epiphany, but a pivotal appreciation of the great trust the Professor elected to bestow upon me.

In the past, my most common emotions had ever been those of rage and fear, but Professor MacMorris's gentle act awoke within my breast a love nearly as violent as my past hatreds. He was my first real friend, and I would give my life for him...and his daughter.

Once Robbie Pratt went home, the Professor said that he had made the boy feel sufficiently guilty for inadvertently causing me harm, and therefore the youth promised that he would not say anything about me in the village. I hoped the boy would be true to his word, though I had serious doubts that he would.

In the days that followed, the Professor and his daughter Eve tended me on a make-shift cot in their cabin, but although my host is medically trained, my fracture baffled him, for the bones refused to knit. Nor would the knife-slash close, though he kept it clean and bandaged. Worse, after the accident by the waterfall, small, bleeding rifts began to appear at the junctures where my creator had first stitched me together.

One day, when Eve was off to town, I told the Professor my story—parts of it, at least.

"Have you ever heard of a man called Victor Frankenstein?" I asked him, fearing he would immediately connect the name with the death of Henry Clerval, but though he had a vague recollection that he had heard of him at some time or other, he could not recall the particulars.

"He was a scientist, but like none other of that description."

"In what way did he differ, Will?"

"Professor, I must now ask you to countenance something so strange that you may think I am either delusive or just plain lying. Victor Frankenstein created me."

He set his chin upon his closed hand and pondered what I had told him. After a moment, he nodded and said, "So that is why your hands, and I presume your feet, are sutured to your limbs?"

"Indeed, yes."

"I would ask where he got them from, but as a former member of the Edinburgh surgical faculty, I am sure that I already know the answer."

"Then you accept what I tell you as true?"

"Will, I have often heard speculation by other scientists that someday man will learn how to create artificial life. I am thinking of a chemist named Waldman, for one—"

"He was one of my creator's teachers!"

"That does not surprise me in the least. I am only curious to know what secrets Victor Frankenstein discovered that made it possible to animate presumably dead tissue."

"It was lightning that struck life into me."

He then asked me if I always experienced difficulty healing from wounds, but I told him that no, I had always been swift to recover from injuries inflicted on me in my woodland travels, and I had indeed suffered several of the same. "This is a strange condition for me," I said.

Together we speculated that there must, after all, be limits to Victor Frankenstein's science, and, though for many years it had made me stronger than any other mortal, its scope is evidently finite, and my poor, misshapen body is beginning to break down.

Now I did not fear death, for after all, I had already contemplated it in the Arctic, but now that I had resolved to devote my life to atonement, I was not yet prepared to come to an end, if mortality could be somehow averted.

Professor MacMorris agreed with me that only the barest minimum of my story should be shared with Eve. She is of an inquisitive mind, but when she soon discovered that most of her questions about me, whether posed to her father or myself, were turned aside or produced but partial, therefore unsatisfactory, answers, she at length let the subject rest.

Her frustrated curiosity was not a bar, though, to the development of a special friendship between us, the source of which their cabin was abundant in, for the Professor owned hundreds of books. Over the years, he had derived much joy in reading to his daughter, but by the time I met them, his failing vision prevented him from doing as he once did. So I assumed the role of story-teller, and entertained both Eve, myself, and often the Professor as well. Tales from history, fanciful adventures, even scientific treatises, delighted us, and when a book or story, short or long, was finished, I found a special pleasure in discussing what we did or did not like about it. Our bond grew as Eve and I discovered that the books she liked best were also my favourites.

"Ah, Willie," she told me, patting me on the arm with her own work-roughened hand, "sometimes I think we are old friends who ha' just met."

Even with my injuries, these were the best days of my life.

While I was more or less recuperating, Eve and I had many conversations on topics that ranged widely, from the state of the government, of which I knew precious little, to art, ethics, and the present level of Scottish jurisprudence. Everything interested her, so that even when the topic was something I was both ignorant of, and essentially uncaring, because of her my curiosity woke and often—it became a kind of game for us—I would search through the many, many volumes of the Professor's library to see what, if anything, had already been written on the topic in question, and, of course, my findings (for her father's library was rarely found wanting, when consulted) became a fit topic for me to read about to her and the Professor, and once I did, we all held forth on whatever opinions we had after hearing the state or condition of the question.

Once only did Eve's curiosity startle me. It was early evening and there was still sufficient after-light for me to read to her (the Professor having gone to bed early); the book that I was sharing with her was rife with dark visions of the Hell envisioned by various members of the early Roman Catholic church. The descriptions of sinners caught up in the avenging fists of an angry deity disturbed me; they were shockingly graphic, all too easy to see in the mind's eye, if I may so characterize the uncomfortable mental pictures the book that I was reading conjured up. I wanted to set the nasty thing aside, but Eve protested.

"I do not like the notion of such vicious retaliation against erring mankind," she declared, "but, Willie, it is so vividly described that I can almost *see* it!"

I did not know what to say. "How is that possible?" I asked. "Have you not been blind since birth?"

"Yes, Willie, I have, but I still see pictures in my mind. Maybe they have nothing in common with the look of things in reality, but it is a comfort of sorts to know I have that, at least."

"Do you ever wish—" I stopped myself, realizing the question was perhaps indelicate. But Eve understood.

"Do I ever wish I had eyes that worked? It's all right, I do not mind you asking."

"Yes, then."

"O' course, Willie, o' course! I do not fret about it, though. But when we lived in Edinburgh, I heard the other Doctors talking, and I remember one of them—Doctor Knox it was—he was theorizing how certain kinds of blindness might someday be curable. So who knows, Willie, maybe I shall yet experience a miracle and I will be able to see you."

Without meaning to, I moaned.

"Why what's the matter, Will? Does your wound hurt?"

"A little, but that is not the reason. If you saw how ugly I am—"

"Now, Willie," Eve bridled, "d' y' think I wouldn't love you no matter what you look like? Y'r my sweet guardian angel!"

Her words comforted me, though the reality of my appearance would be a far more severe test of her loyalty than she could possibly imagine. I hoped fervently that such a time would never come; the likelihood of her seeing again was, of course, extremely improbable, but I suddenly felt wretched for harbouring such a selfish thought.

* * * *

One night, I had a bad dream.

I was used to having nightmares about the murders that I have committed, yet this was the first time that I had ever dreamed of Justine Moritz's wrongful execution. The last time when I set eyes on her, I had hidden myself at the edge of the forest a little distance from the gallows. Justine went to her death with serene composure, a Bible clutched to her bosom. Some of the rabble gathered there regarded her with stony hatred, and a few shouted vile things. But Victor Frankenstein was there, too, with the rest of his family, and their faces showed compassion and one of them even shed tears.

In my dream, I rushed into the crowd and confessed my guilt. Most of them ignored me, but not Frankenstein. Facing me, his eyes ablaze with hatred, he snarled, "Villain! Though my bones lay in Arctic ice, yet shall I return and be revenged—depend upon it!"

I woke with a shudder, and dared not sleep again.

* * * *

Next morning, as I sat by the cabin enjoying September sun straggling through the over-hanging branches, I sensed that there was someone watching me.

Looking about, I saw him some distance away. His earth-brown garment blended with the forest, so I did not discover him till he moved. His steps were slow and jerky. He must be lame, I thought. He leaned on a rough crutch fashioned from a thick piece of wood caked with leaves and daubs of stuff I later learned was peat.

I felt a hand upon my shoulder. "Yes, Professor," I said, "we have a visitor."

"Which direction?"

"I will lead you to him."

"Nae. Aim me true, I'll find th' way."

I perceived it as a point of pride, so I did what he asked. The Professor made his way to the newcomer; they conversed briefly, then my friend returned to my side.

"'Tis a priest. He'd like to meet you."

"Why? I don't know him."

"Robbie must have broken his word, and blabbed about y'."

"Well, there is no harm, I suppose. The man seems so very frail."

"I'll have t' take your word for 't." The Professor beckoned; the priest hobbled over. I wondered how old he was. His hair was grey-white; a network of crinkles bracketed brown eyes and his chin was covered with a trim grey beard.

"My name," he said, "is Father Naman. I come from Dunkeld." (A village about fourteen miles south and to the east of Pitlochry, the Professor later told me.) As the priest spoke, he looked at me with an oddly focused curiosity, but at least he did not cringe at my ugliness.

"What do you want of me?" I asked.

"I had business in Pitlochry," he said, his voice clearer and easier to understand than the Professor's glottal stops. "A lad I met there told me about a giant in the woods who had been hurt in an accident." (So much for Robbie Pratt's promise, I thought.) "It struck me that this injured person might need my assistance, and now that I see you, it is evident that you are in considerable pain, so, with your permission—"

He rested the palm of his hand lightly upon my breast. To my surprise and gratitude, the aches inflicted by my injuries began to ebb away. I was astonished that his touch could banish my suffering, yet more wondrous, this cleric not only did not shrink from gazing upon me, he seemed to look into my heart with unflinching concern.

SPIRITUAL COMFORT

(Father Naman)

I was some distance away, moving, as ever, slowly and unsteadily. Sciatica is a misery. Each step I take with my right leg threatens to pitch me down, so I must cling to the "stick" that I had fashioned into an *ersatz* cane.

When he first saw me, he was sitting on a wooden bench in front of a small log cabin. As the Pratt boy had said, he was huge, ill-proportioned, ugly. The lad called him a monster, but as I drew near, whatever aversion I might have felt was over-ridden by an acute sense of the agony that he was in—pain of the spirit more than that of the flesh.

A priest is trained to peer beneath the surface, and for all my premonitory feelings, I could not set aside the conviction that of all the wretched creatures I have met upon God's earth, this poor being, misshapen and grotesque though he was, struck me not as a monster, but rather a victim—a suffering one.

Touching his chest, I drew upon those healing energies my spiritual schooling enables me to harness. As his aches abated, he stared at me in surprise.

"How is it possible," he asked, "for a stranger's hand to take away my pain?"

"It is old knowledge from the East," I said. "But your soul, as well, is troubled."

"I am not sure that I have one."

"Were that so, my touch would have accomplished nothing."

"Well, then," he admitted, "I am afraid of having a soul."

"Why is that?"

"I fear retribution for my sins."

To that there is but one answer, which I told to him. "We must hate the sin, but not the sinner."

"Your counsel soothes me."

"Laddie," Professor MacMorris interposed, "all of us who live possess immortal spirits, and yours has been sorely taxed. Still, I am more concerned about the present condition of your body. We can not wait any longer for Captain Walton to join us, y' are in great need o' medical attention."

"What must I do?" the giant asked.

"I will take you t' Edinburgh." MacMorris turned to his daughter. "Eve, can you fend for a few days on your own till I return?"

"And why shouldn't I come along with y'?"

"And why should you?" The Professor's tone was suddenly quite frosty.

"Because," she said with the suggestion of a temper ready to flare up, "I want to pay a visit to my mother!"

Some argument now passed between father and daughter, but though they wrangled vociferously, it struck me that whatever reasons the Professor was putting forth to prevent his daughter from coming along with them did not express his real objections.

At length the girl got her way, and that is when the creature voiced his concerns.

"How may I travel with you?" he protested. "Those who see me will never tolerate my presence."

That is when I spoke up. "I will find you a garment that will cover you from head to foot. We will travel at night."

"We?" The creature was mystified. "Mustn't you return to your duties at Dunkeld?"

"I am on Sabbatical."

"A carriage for four will cost a wee bit," the Professor mused.

"I have taken a vow," I said, "but not of poverty."

The following night found us all en route to Edinburgh, Scotland's teeming capital of dirt, sin and squalor.

EN ROUTE

Father Naman was as good as his word. He found a large home-spun robe with a hood that I could pinch closed to hide my face.

I sensed unusual tension between Eve and the Professor. Normally they got along lovingly, but from the scraps of talk I heard between them now, I realized that there was one sore point dividing them, and that concerned Eve's mother, whom the girl wanted to visit in Edinburgh.

It was abundantly clear that Eve's father did not want her to have anything to do with her mother. I did not know why, though later, in Edinburgh, I found out the particulars.

We did not start out on our south-ward junket till well after dark.

As our carriage rumbled into town, I voiced misgivings to the Professor. "Edinburgh," I said, "is one of Europe's chief medical centers, yet I do not think that its physicians will possess the skills needed to treat my condition."

"Och, laddie, there is one man here that I know who just might succeed."

"But who could possibly comprehend the science that made me?" Even as I said it, I wished that I could call back the words; Father Naman, after all, was not privy to my bizarre history. But then I relaxed, for I heard the priest snore, and knew that he had not heard me.

In answer to my question, Professor MacMorris chuckled, though not altogether pleasantly. "Willie, I daresay ye've never met the likes o' Doctor Robert Knox."

PART TWO

In Edinburgh

A VERY STRANGE PATIENT

(Andrew Napier)

I am old like Cardinal Wolsey, not in calendar years, but weary from long service to Doctor Robert Knox, whom some have called "Knox, the infamous butcher," but that was some time later than the events which I am here describing.

I began as one of the Doctor's medical students, but, lacking the mind and discipline for success in that profession, by starts and turns I devolved, or perhaps degenerated into becoming his Major-domo, not that my duties were limited to the homely (by that I mean innocent) tasks of house-keeping.

The Doctor's residence and teaching theatre are situated in the district known as Surgeon's Square, Edinburgh, a place that students call Auld Reekie, thanks to the noxious fumes produced by hundreds of coal- and wood-burning stoves that make the air easier to choke upon than to breathe.

Our town is a place of extremes and contradictions. Its bloody history is commingled with its geography. The long, thin boundaries of the mid-town district are defined by a volcanic ridge that runs a tad more than a mile from Edinburgh Castle, sloping east-ward to Holyrood House, which stands close by a series of up-stepping ridges that mount south and west to Arthur's Seat, the old mountain that, like the Castle, dominates our sky-line. Marshy grass-land further to the south has helped discourage the English from invading us on more than one occasion, while our northern border is guarded by a great lake that may appeal to the eye, but never the nose, for winter and summer, slops and chamber-pots are emptied from high windows, and woe to the visitor who does not heed the ominous cry accompanying such activity, "Gardy-loo!" (A corruption from the French phrase, "Gardez l'eau," meaning "watch out for the water.") Much of this jettisoned effluent runs down the steeply-sloping alleys of the old town to drain into the lake. Unwanted kittens and puppies are also thrown in there, and worser things, I fear. There is talk now of draining the lake and putting up new homes to the north for some of our more affluent citizens. While I have neither sympathy nor interest in what they do, expanding the town limits seems a good idea, in that it may reduce the overcrowding. Because of the narrowness of Edinburgh along its north-south boundaries, with the Pentland hills and Arthur's Seat on the west and east, the only way to accommodate the demand for more housing has been to construct the tallest buildings in Europe. We call them "lands," some of them as high as fifteen stories. Pity the top-most tenants, doomed to exhausting climbs past garbage-strewn landings that no one keeps clean, save perhaps the rats. Someday, I fear, fire will sweep it all away. Perhaps only then could we build a cleaner, purer city.

Well, an end to my rambling. If you know anything about medicine, you have heard of Doctor Robert Knox, though probably not in detail. He lives within—and relishes!—the tempest's eye. Tall, imposing, used to having his own way, he affects expensive trousers, ruffled shirts, exquisitely-tailored morning coats; in his cravat he sports a diamond stick-pin, and over his left eye he generally wears a black patch that makes him look more like a dandified pirate than a surgeon. Despite sullen murmurs in certain quarters of town devoted to things spiritual, for which he has scant patience, Doctor Knox is much in demand socially. He is also oddly (so I think) popular with the ladies. There is about him virtually an electrical aura; his features are mobile, especially when he is lecturing on anatomy to students who hang upon his every word. And students he has by the hundreds, more so than any other medical tutor in the district, which contributes to the suspicion and jealousy with which he is regarded by his colleagues. But his fame is unarguably earned. His anatomical theories alone place him at the fore-front of his profession.

Doctor K. is curator and founder of the museum of the Royal College of Surgeons here in town. He has upward of five hundred students, who jam the operating theatre to hear his lectures and absorb the dynamic power he radiates as he performs exacting autopsies, in which he often compares human anatomy to that of various animal species.

His success, however, has been attended by one huge problem. It is enormously difficult for him and all other medical lecturers to obtain bodies to dissect. This ongoing need is the key element of Doctor Knox's contempt for what he dubs "Religionists," his ironic echo of the name for the cottage industry of "Resurrectionists" that sprang up to provide us with new-buried corpses.

A "Resurrectionist" is, of course, a fancy title for a grave-robber, and those folk are so assiduous in supplying our needs, that it is not uncommon for a grieving family to set watch in the cemetery to prevent Resurrectionists from snatching away the dead; this grim vigil is maintained for about two weeks, after which decay renders the body useless to the anatomist.

Now before you condemn this traffic in bodies (though I do admit that I also possess negative feelings about it), do try to understand the anatomist's problem. According to Scottish law, the only bodies legally available are an occasional pauper without kin, or executed criminals—and the number of public executions, from an historic perspective, has been dwindling. As for relatives dying in hospital, they are buried according to church ritual, and a surgeon's appeal to donate the remains for the good of science falls on ears not just deaf, but hostile, for the notion of loved ones being sliced open for students to gape at is deemed to be thoroughly unholy.

Now let me turn to the business at hand. One night, my principal was entertaining a distaff companion upstairs in his private quarters. Paterson, our janitor, had the day off, so Doctor Knox assigned me to late duty in the dissecting laboratory in the cellar, where bodies often are brought to us after dark. Paterson cannot be trusted to do the arithmetic accurately, so I was busy trying to bring the ledger up to date. I had closed my eyes to rest them from the candle's tiring flicker, but the moment, I fear, became perhaps an hour as I slumped and dozed against a rough wooden trestle where I had been working.

I was wakened by the tingle of the bell outside a door which opens onto a narrow, dark (even in daylight) alley-way. I supposed it must be one of our usual Resurrectionists with a delivery. I went to see who it was, but was ill-prepared for what greeted me.

In my taper's indistinct glimmer, I perceived four figures, one of them a girl. Two wore cowled robes; one of these, whose face was hidden, was gigantic. The last of the four I recognized. Here was no Resurrectionist!

"Professor MacMorris!" I exclaimed. "I thought that you had moved away."

"So I did," he replied, "but I have returned with a friend much in need of medical attention. Andrew, kindly summon Doctor Knox."

"At *this* hour?"

"Daylight is mine enemy," the giant growled. He lowered his cowl, revealing features so hideous that I reeled and almost fainted. Doctor Knox's wrath seemed a lesser evil than this monstrosity!

Still, I hesitated. "Gentlemen ..." then, not to appear impolite, added, "Miss ... Doctor Knox is not available to-night for any reason." This was not strictly true; I had not been given specific instructions, yet I well knew how imprudent—I might go so far as to say dangerous—it would be for me to disturb Doctor Knox in his bed-chamber when he was entertaining womanly company.

"This is a medical emergency!" the Professor argued. He looked as if he might say more, but the smaller man in robes patted his arm and stepped forward.

"I am a man of God," he said. "Take me to Knox. I will speak with him."

Considering Doctor K.'s contempt for clergy, I feared his presence would only aggravate things, but though his demeanour was mild, I got the distinct impression that this priest was accustomed to compliance, so, not without a sotto voce groan, I guided him up the cellar steps to the front vestibule and from there to the stairs that led to Doctor Knox's chambers.

Doctor K.'s reaction was precisely what I had expected. He threatened to throw me out of my job on the morrow, and out of a window within the next ten seconds. What saved me from that dire fate was that he took a breath, and in that brief interval I swiftly stated that surely the strangest patient he would ever set eyes upon waited below.

He growled for particulars, so I began to describe the giant, but the priest interrupted me. "The patient," he said, "is waiting in the alley-way with one of your former colleagues."

"Do I know you, sir?" Doctor K.'s bristly tone would have warned off any of his students, but the cleric, not the least bit cowed, produced a folded envelope.

"Kindly peruse this, sir. I have taken the liberty of describing the patient's condition."

Doctor K. snatched it away from him and began reading, squinting for want of spectacles which, I guessed, had been cast aside with his clothes, for he came to us clad in a black silken robe, one of many that he possessed. When he raised his gaze from the missive, I was startled at how swiftly he had passed from menacing to amiable. "Andrew, you did well to summon me! Escort the patient to an examination room."

I lost no time in doing what I had been told. Escorting the patient and his friends to one of the larger exam-rooms, I waited for a long nerve-wracking time with them. The giant's face, even at rest, was dreadful to behold.

Doctor Knox kept us waiting so long that I suspect he went ahead and completed the business that he was engaged upon before being interrupted.

1 MEET DOCTOR KNOX

Andrew Napier, the man who greeted us, had a triangular face that drew down to a narrow chin which just missed being a sharp point. His blood-shot brown eyes squinted repeatedly, as if he were unused to the light. His tousled black hair was shot with grey, which matched his drab jacket and trousers.

He brought us to a wood-paneled room. Its pale green walls were covered with medical charts and anatomical illustrations. He took a chair as far away from me as possible and studied his fidgety fingers with singular attention. Time passed slowly, but he kept silent. When the Professor, who had been growing more and more impatient, finally asked him to go and see why Doctor Knox was keeping us waiting so very long, Napier, nodding with evident relief, said he would do so at once, and immediately left the room.

We did not see him again until, at long last, the Doctor himself appeared.

I had no clear notion what to expect. Professor MacMorris had assured me that Doctor Knox was a scientific genius, and that made me think of Victor Frankenstein, for, after all, my creator was, up to that time, the only man I had ever known who fitted that description. Now Frankenstein's aspect and demeanour combined elements both of high romance and intellectual fervour. Slim, yet sinewy, with undeniably handsome features (their absence in me does not prevent my recognizing them in him), he had the combined air of a scholar and poet.

Well, intellect Doctor Knox certainly possesses, but in no other way does he resemble my personal hero-daemon, Victor Frankenstein. Instead, the strange dandy who strode into the chamber where we had been waiting was a muscular man with broad shoulders and a large, mostly bald head bracketed by long dark side-boards, I think that is what they are called. He looked to be in his mid-to-late thirties, and was clad like one of William Congreve's fops, for he sported diamonds mounted in gold as a fixative for his bright red cravat. His coat and trousers were costly in appearance, but overly adorned with silver ornaments, an ornate watch chain, and so many rings on his fingers that I wondered how he could possibly palpate his patients. All this, plus a black patch that covered his left eye; the other, though, was uncommonly sharp as it swept over each of his visitor's countenances, coming to rest at last on mine.

He nodded to Father Naman, then, in a voice as gruff as his manner, addressed the Professor. "Abel, do introduce me to your interesting friend."

"His name is Will," the Professor replied. "Willie Pratt."

"Indeed?" The way he said it, the way he looked at me was vaguely disturbing—but then the Doctor doffed his supercilious manner like a cape and began to study me. "Mr. Pratt, may I examine you?"

I told him yes. With his assistant Napier's help, I was placed supine upon a long treatment table and Doctor Knox began to take measurements, to poke and prod and listen to my heart and lungs. After several minutes of this, he told me that I could sit up again. As I did, the physician circled round his desk, took a seat, and pointed to Father Naman. "According to the account this priest gave me earlier, you are—how may I best put it?—a *manufactured* creation."

That startled me, of course, but I said that this was true, expecting him to ridicule the notion. But he did not.

"I have toyed with such a possibility," he said. "Yet my profession places me at the other end of the spectrum from he who made you. What do you know of his methods?"

"Never mind tha!" the Professor objected. "What is your diagnosis?"

"Abel," Doctor Knox replied crisply, "I require an answer to my query."

I did not know that much about the process of my "birth," but I told him what I could about the gleaned limbs and parts assembled that became me. I also said that I knew it was lightning that shocked me into life.

"That is what I had suspected," said Doctor Knox, his lips working from side to side. "Yes, Abel, I see your impatience, so here is my answer. The science that fashioned—Will—is altogether remarkable, yet mortality claims us all. In my opinion, the injuries he has recently sustained have touched off a process of cellular degeneration at a rate uncommon for living flesh." With a grim head-shake, he turned to me. "I am afraid, sir, that strong as you are, you already half-lay in your coffin."

"For God's sake, Robert," the Professor exclaimed, "isn't there anything that you can do to help him?"

"Something can be done, of course, for his broken leg, and to stanch that knife-wound. Now in theory, I perceive a way to reverse, or at least retard, the degenerative process, but in practice such a procedure has never been performed. How could it? Never before has there been such a need."

"But you will do it, of course!"

"Abel, it is only a theory, and what I would have to do would be too painful to perform upon any living man."

I grasped Doctor Knox's arm in my great fist. "I will endure *all pain!*"

The surgeon glared at me. "Release my arm." Though two feet and a bit shorter than I am, in his own way he was quite formidable. I let him go. He stepped up to me; I was still seated on the treatment table, so he could look more or less directly into my eyes. "I will make myself clearer. I would have to cut you open while you are wide awake."

I said I would suffer it.

"Not once, mind you, but two or three times. It may take weeks, for you must recover before going on to the next stage. I do not know how much surgery your system will be able to tolerate."

"I am already under sentence of death."

His gaze was both speculative and concerned. "That is true. If I do nothing, sooner or later you shall succumb. Yet this undertaking— make no mistake!—amounts to a series of autopsies upon a living patient. The chance of failure is great, the work will be arduous and time-consuming, and my schedule is crammed as tight as a haggis-sack. But," he added, with a sudden startling grin, "I am the only surgeon who could even conceive of such an approach, and who has better than half a chance of succeeding." Then his smile became a frown. "If I try to undertake this, what is to prevent you from injuring me when the pain grows more terrible than you can imagine?"

The Professor interrupted. "Why does this trouble you, Robert? Surely you will anaesthetize him!"

"Surely I will not."

"But that is utterly barbaric!"

Doctor Knox vented a deep sigh. "Abel, you are gifted at dispensing remedies for minor ailments, but we are now dealing with problems beyond the scope of your comprehension. Do not presume to dictate what I may or may not be able to do!"

That stirred Eve to utter a harsh rejoinder, but her father shushed her. Father Naman murmured something to them that I could not hear, but it seemed to calm them. They settled back in their seats and said nothing further.

During this brief interchange, Doctor Knox watched and waited. Once it was clear that they had resolved their issues, at least for the time being, he turned back to me and again asked how I could be sure I would not injure him during the painful surgeries he proposed to undertake on my behalf.

"You may tie me down. I shall regard the agony I must endure as partial expiation for my sins."

A sour smile. "That sentiment will sit well with the town's church elders."

"*You must tell no one!*" My shout made Napier fall off his chair.

"Calm yourself," the Doctor counseled. "You will be accorded the customary medical confidentiality. But are you able to pay for my time and surgical supplies?"

The Professor rose. "Robert, this is a personal favour to me."

"Indeed? And am I indebted to you, Abel?"

"Think of two names, Robert," he replied. "One of them—" He whispered to Doctor Knox. "The other one, I should not have to mention."

Doctor Knox glared at him, but turned to his assistant. "Andrew, tomorrow you will go out and purchase the strongest leather straps you can find."

TWO NAMES

(Andrew Napier)

It all sounded strange to me, but, after all, what could one of Doctor K.'s failed medical students really know? I supposed that he had a sound reason for the bizarre ordeal he meant to inflict upon the patient.

Professor MacMorris's secret hold on my principal, though, was not a mystery to me, for I was sitting near enough to hear the name that he murmured into Doctor Knox's ear. It was "Mary." Which meant, of course, that he was reminding him of the late Mary Tennant, a sweet-tempered lassie of the evening. A lovely young girl she had been, much sought after by students who were determined to study distaff anatomy in a more practical fashion than what mere text-books could offer them.

Now before I may continue with this explanation, I must needs introduce you to a pair of hateful brutes named William Burke and Willie Hare. No Scotsmen, that pair. Burke was a thick clod from County Cork, Ireland, while Hare was a wily ferret from Londonderry. They had crossed the Irish Sea and went to Linlithgow, not far from Edinburgh, to work on the Union Canal. But labour of that sort was way too strenuous for the likes of them, so Burke became a cobbler and settled into a lodging house where Hare had taken up with a woman named Helen MacDougal who ran the place. It was in Tanner's Close in the West Port (slum) district.

Burke and Hare began to bring us bodies. Now so far as Doctor Knox was concerned, they were just another pair of Resurrectionists, but I had grave (no pun intended) doubts upon the subject. If a man keeps his ears open and his mouth shut, he learns a thing or two. One of the facts that I had found out about Resurrectionists is that they formed their own labour union and parceled out assignments based on seniority and, to a lesser extent, merit. Now membership in this fell society was strictly restricted to Scots. Had Burke or Hare entered any cemetery within a ten-mile radius of Edinburgh and tried to dig up newly-buried cadavers, it is likely that our students would soon be dissecting *them*. And besides, setting spades to six feet of earth is hard work, a detestable concept to that pair.

I was therefore convinced that wherever they found the bodies they brought us, it was not from the depths of sanctified earth...

Late one night, Burke and Hare rang our bell. The body that they wheeled over to us in a cart was that of Mary Tennant. It happened to be one of those infrequent occasions when Doctor Knox himself was working in the lab.

When I perceived the identity of the deceased, I tried to catch the eye of my employer, but he ignored my worried efforts and personally paid off Burke and Hare.

When I wheeled her into the teaching theatre the next morning, the collective gasp that went up from the students startled me and caught the attention of Professor MacMorris, who was in the chamber conferring with Doctor K. The Professor certainly witnessed what followed.

This was the only time in my memory when Doctor K's students tried to stand up to him. One of them even shouted that we must call the authorities at once, for Mary must have been murdered. But the anatomist, confronting them head-on, raised his voice, something which he seldom did. "Things we see and do in this room," he declared, "are subject to the same code of silence that rules us as physicians. Why are you so upset? Because she died young? Was her life more precious than that old palsied man you took apart last week? Was that one easier because you did not know his name? Did that lacuna enable you to act the part of medical professionals? For acting it must have been, judging by your unprofessional attitude toward this specimen!" Mere written words cannot convey the acidulous contempt with which Doctor K., his face livid, his free eye glaring, delivered this invective.

And yet with reflection, I realize that he must have been acting, as well. Otherwise, on the night the giant came to us, why would

Professor MacMorris's mere mention of Mary Tennant's name have secured Doctor Knox's cooperation?

As for the other name, he did not say it aloud, but I was certain that it was Patsy Kensit.

SCOTTISH ACCOMMODATIONS

I am not sure how or when I was exposed to that prejudice about the Scots being a stingy folk. If it be peasant wisdom, it does not appertain to the Professor or his feisty child. Yet when it comes to architecture, Edinburgh's spatial parsimony surely qualifies. The room that Andrew guided me to was not just small, its proportions were so cramped its designer must have been determined to use as little as he could of the available building materials.

The chamber was one flight closer to the sky above Doctor Knox's private apartment, and it was gained by negotiating—in my case, with severe difficulty—a spiral stairwell wound round a core so tight that I could scarcely breathe as I worked my way upward.

Once in the room, I sat down on a narrow cot suspended by chains from a rough wall of dingy plaster, but the thing broke under my weight.

"Oh, dear!" Andrew lamented, offering me a hand so that I could stand up. Considering how afraid of me he was, his gesture touched me. "I will try to get that fixed for you."

"Never mind that! Find him another room!" Father Naman emerged from the staircase.

"Begging your pardon," Andrew cringed, "but Doctor Knox told me to keep him where the students would not see him."

"It's all right," I said, sitting down at a small corner desk. "I can manage here. I shall need candles and, if possible, some books."

Head waggling, Napier assured me that he would do everything he could, and took his leave. As soon as he was gone, Father Naman walked over and, resting his walking stick against the wall, placed his hand on the spot where the carpenter's knife had ripped me open. The wound had flared up as I climbed the steep stairs to the attic, but his touch took away the pain.

"How did you know that I hurt? Did my face show it?"

"No," he responded. "You are good at masking pain. But after watching you for long hours in the carriage, and waiting for Doctor Knox to examine you, I perceived how you silently endure the unendurable. Now hush while I balance your chakras."

It was a new word to me, but I did not question him; his touch was answer enough; it soothed and comforted; that was sufficient. When he was finished, he squinted his eyes so they almost disappeared as he removed his spectacles to wipe them. As he did, he asked how I felt.

"Better," I answered, "but it has been a long day, and the ride was rough. Where is the Professor and Eve?"

"They are provided for. Knox said he would get them a dormitory room."

"What about you?"

"I will go to St. Giles. It is Edinburgh's principal cathedral, and it is open day and night. A pallet will be provided for me there." He gestured to my cot, now resting on the floor. "Will you be able to manage on that?"

"I have slept on worse," I said. But before laying down, I had to ask him how he had found out that I was a laboratory creation.

"I heard a few odd remarks pass between you and Professor MacMorris, so I asked him out-right, and he told me about it."

That surprised me almost as much as the priest's knowledge, but I was too exhausted to pursue it. I sat on the cot and expected that he would bid me good night, but he remained seated at the desk, regarding me with evident concern. I asked him what was troubling him, but, instead of replying, he studied his hands. I repeated my question.

"I am debating whether I have any right to say anything to you about this thing."

"What thing?"

"The thing that you mean to do. Have you truly thought it through?"

"I have no choice, Father."

"Man always has a choice." Resettling his spectacles on his nose, he set his chair closer to the cot and sat down beside me. "I grant you that I am no expert in traditional medicine, but I agree with Professor MacMorris—what Knox proposes to do to you strikes me as horrifying."

"I am not looking forward to it. But I meant what I told him."

"That business about expiating sin?"

"Father, if you possessed my self-knowledge, you would not disagree."

"Perhaps, but I am a priest, which means that I am trained to suspect the subtle snares the Devil devises to tempt sinners."

He was beginning to irritate me. "I am not deluded, Father! My sins are all too real!"

"I am not saying that they are not," he reassured me. "What I suggest, instead, is that your plan to undergo Doctor Knox's scalpel may not be penitence, but may stem from a martyr's pride."

Such a thought never would have occurred to me. Yet in all truth, I could not be sure that Father Naman was not right. "How may I know whether this be true or not?"

"My son, there is one way that might guide you through this crisis."

"Well, you took away my pain, so I trust you. Guide me, then."

He nodded. "If I am able, I will. But first, you must confess your sins. I will evaluate them, and define the terms of your penance. Will you thus be guided?"

"Must I share those horrors?"

"As your Confessor, do understand that I will be sworn to secrecy. I may not repeat what you tell me, not even to save my own life."

"Then let us begin."

CONFESSIONAL

(Father Naman)

I knelt beside him. Had we been in church, each of us would have occupied a separate small booth, but he was not Catholic, so I did not see that our unorthodox arrangement mattered.

"In my faith," I began, "sins vary in nature and degree. There is original sin, there are those we term venial, and then there are mortal sins."

"Mine," he said, "are the latter."

"No sin but one is unforgiveable."

"The exception, I suppose, must be murder."

"You suppose wrong. It is written in the Book of Matthew that the only unpardonable sin is an unclean soul that utters blasphemy against the Holy Spirit."

"Then," the creature asked, "there is still hope for me?"

"Perhaps. Whom did you kill?"

He shaded his eyes so that I could not see him (or, for that matter, so that he could not see me, either). "Three times I have murdered. There was a fourth in the Arctic, the man who slashed me. But that was self-defense, and I do not feel remorse or any sense of responsibility about him. However, I killed a man, a woman, and a child, and those murders I repent ... though that last one was accidental... almost."

I began to reply to that, but he stopped me.

"If you interrupt me now, I will not have the heart to continue."

"Very well. Three murders. Is there anything else that troubles your conscience?"

He nodded. "Three other deaths are also my fault, though they were not directly brought about by my hands. Yet they are a consequence of mine actions."

I withdrew a flask that I kept within my robes. I swallowed a generous portion of scotch whisky, and settled back to hear what he was about to tell me.

First he spoke of the death of Henry Clerval.

"A familiar name," I said. "Wasn't there an arrest made for it?"

"They accused Victor Frankenstein, my creator. Do you know anything about him?"

"The alleged perpetrator, I recall, was someone named Victor Frankenstein."

"Yes," he said. 'And now you know my own name."

"What? He gave you his name?"

"No. I took it for myself. The only thing he ever gave me was the curse of existence."

I felt pity for him, but I perserved. "How did the murder case against him turn out?"

"He became quite ill. Eventually they let him go."

"But why did you murder Henry Clerval?"

He glared. "Father, there was a time when I owned gentler feelings. But when my creator destroyed the woman meant to be my wife, I became—perhaps irrationally—vengeful."

I was utterly shocked. "Victor Frankenstein killed someone dear to you?!"

"He ripped her apart!" His fist struck the table; it cracked. It was the first time I had witnessed his formidable strength. He forced himself to be calm. "Frankenstein," he continued, "promised to fashion a mate for me, but went back on his word, and destroyed my wife-to-be. In a legal sense, however, he had committed no crime, for she never drew the first breath of life."

"So you killed Henry Clerval in revenge?"

"Frankenstein's wife, too. I strangled her the night they were married."

I sought strength. This confession was an ordeal. "When you did these sinful acts, were you glad that you had done them?"

"No. I hated myself even more than Frankenstein."

"What about the child you slew?"

"I did not know who he was. I saw him running with all the sportiveness of childhood, and thought here is one too small, too new to dislike me. I imagined that he could become my friend, but as soon as he beheld me, he screamed and called me ogre. I said I would not hurt him, but he struggled and cursed and warned me that I would be punished by his father, who was a syndic named Frankenstein."

"So that is when you killed him?"

"No! I grasped his throat to stop him from uttering epithets that brought despair to my heart. But suddenly there he lay, dead at my feet!"

"Were you sorry that you had killed him?"

"I shall not further stain my soul by lying. My heart swelled with hellish triumph, for I had authored an act of desolation that would make my creator despair. Yet when I saw the locket glittering on William's small breast, I was softened and attracted by the portrait of the lovely woman it contained. For a few moments I gazed with delight on her dark eyes, fringed by deep lashes, and her lovely lips, but then my rage returned, for I was forever deprived of such delights."

But nothing that I told the priest seemed to change his mind.

"Your deeds, horrible though they were," Father Naman declared, "brought nearly as much pain to their perpetrator as they did to the victims. I do not think they require further penance under Doctor Knox's knife."

"There are three deaths I caused indirectly," I argued. "I have not told you of them yet."

"Then do so," he told me.

"The most recent was my creator. Victor Frankenstein chased me literally to the earth's end, and died on shipboard near the North Pole."

"Of natural causes?"

"I suppose his heart gave out."

"You tormented him," the priest said, "but you may claim the same aggrievance in reverse. I do not think his death is your fault. Let it go. Tell me about the second death for which you blame yourself." I saw him take another few swallows of scotch.

"Frankenstein's father," I confessed. "He succumbed, I suppose, to cumulative grief."

"But this, too, is a tragedy that I do not believe you are responsible for...which leaves but one death unaccounted for..."

I looked at the priest. How forgiving he seemed—yet how could he forgive me? A long pause. At last, I said, "Father, you must be weary. Let us meet again tomorrow."

"I believe that means that this last death troubles you more than all of the others combined," Father Naman said. "Am I right?"

I wished he was less perceptive. "Yes," I told him. "Her name was Justine Moritz. She was a servant and something of an adopted daughter to the Frankensteins."

"How did Justine die?"

"They hanged her."

The priest made the sign of the cross. "What do they claim that she had done?"

"They blamed her for the death of the child, Frankenstein's youngest brother, the one that I had unintentionally killed."

"Tell me how this happened."

"Soon after the death of the child, I came upon a woman who was sleeping in the woods. She was young, and though she was not as beautiful as the woman in the portrait, still she was attractive enough. Later I learned her name. I imagined this damsel smiling at everyone but me, and though I knew her not, I hated her. I approached her unperceived and put the boy's locket in the folds of her dress, where it was found by the authorities. They said she killed him for the locket, and hanged her for it. I now deplore my malice, but in those days, as you know, I was an angry, tormented creature." A long and palpable silence passed before I spoke again. "You need not tell me that my crimes are unforgivable."

"Four murders are a heavy burden…for you killed Justine as surely as if you had choked her with your own hands!" He rose to his feet, fetched his walking-stick and, instead of leaning on it as he usually did, he pointed it at me and proclaimed, "Here, confessor, is my judgment. Those whom you strangled are the dreadful consequences of that anguish bequeathed to you by Victor Frankenstein. He alone is responsible for the lust for revenge that grew in your bosom. These murders are expiated in the eyes of Our Merciful Lord…but not this poor innocent girl's death! This is the greatest sin that you have confessed." He stared into my eyes for one silent moment and then, lowering his walking stick, settled his weight against it with a sigh. He drained his flask, then spoke once more. "Doctor Knox's scalpel is, after all, a suitable means to atone for Justine's wrongful death."

I looked to him for some shred of comfort, but he turned his back on me and abruptly left the chamber, leaving me alone and upset.

MY FIRST OPERATION

Next day dragged by with nothing but guilt to occupy my mind. Andrew had not yet honoured my request for something to read. The day slowly slipped away, the light was beginning to fade, and I had concluded that I was altogether abandoned and forgotten, relegated to tedium without end in this cramped attic oubliette. Suddenly, however, Andrew appeared. He was laden with a double armful of books and, perched precariously atop the pile, a tray bearing a bowl of soup and a small dish of cold meat and greens.

"I am sorry that I could not bring you more food," he apologized, "but Doctor Knox has restricted what you consume today."

"Why is that?"

"He is performing the first operation to-night, and he does not want your stomach engaged in digesting when he does. So do eat right away."

I was not hungry, but promised him that I would do so. Before I could thank him for the reading matter or for the food, he was gone. I would have invited him to stay a while, but it was evident that Andrew did not find me compelling company. Still, I was grateful to him; the varying nature of the books he had brought me suggested that he did put some thought into what I might possibly wish to read. Medical texts there were, of course, for there must be many of those in the house, but he had also brought me fiction by native Scots, some of which I knew, whereas others were new to me. He had even included a slim volume of poetry by Robert Burns.

I selected this book and sat down to the broth and platter which I have since learned is called Ploughman's Lunch (short for luncheon, which is obvious, of course, but I set it down because I have always been fascinated with language and its "short-cuts" (I devised that term this very moment!)

"The doc'r wants y'. Folla me."

I was resting on my cot with eyes shut when I was wakened by a harsh unfamiliar voice. Looking up, I saw a dour knot of a man with grizzled dark hair, beard and moustache. He wore a butcher's apron spattered with brownish splotches.

"Who are you? Where's Andrew?"

"'e's off duty, I'm Pat'r'son. C'm alo'g, folla me."

This was the janitor; Andrew had mentioned him to me earlier. I stood up. When he saw how far above his head I towered, he stumbled back against the wall and told me to keep my distance. I willed myself to hold my temper. Andrew, you see, though I made him nervous, treated me with consideration and respect, but this grizzled janitor, my instinct told me, regarded me with hatred and contempt.

He started down the narrow stairs. I waited a few seconds before following. As before, the downward spiral proved an uncomfortable squeeze.

Paterson led me to the surgery and left me there with Doctor Knox, who wore the physician's traditional white gown.

"I have given your case careful thought," he said. "Your creator's methods depended in part upon the generative power of electricity. To that end, I have ordered special equipment. When it arrives, we shall begin the operations."

"Andrew told me that you would begin operating on me to-night."

"Yes," he nodded, "but nothing major. Your broken leg ought to be fairly simple to repair." He handed me a quart of scotch whisky. "Drink this neat, then lay on the operating table. I hope that that is enough, by the way. I thought that a quart might be pertinent to your size."

I opened the bottle and swallowed some of the liquor; it was sweet and fiery, with a startling after-taste of iodine and peat.

"An interesting flavour, is it not? It is made by the sea-side, and that contributes to its unique character."

"I do like it," I said, "but I thought I was not going to be anaesthetized?"

"That is true for the operations to come, but tonight is a comparatively minor procedure, so finish the bottle and lie down."

I did so. He strapped me down with a set of strong leather thongs that Andrew had evidently procured for the purpose.

For the next hour or thereabouts, Doctor Knox cut into me. The scotch dulled my senses, but it was still difficult to endure the pain. After a while, he summoned Paterson and told him to bring me another quart of scotch.

"Make it two bottles," I growled.

THE NIGHT LIFE
OF EDINBURGH

I feared that after what I had revealed about my past, I would never see Father Naman again, for I was convinced that he must now detest me.

The day dragged by slowly. Andrew brought chicken broth and haggis, which I'd come to like. It was served in what he described as the traditional fashion with, as near as I can render what he told me, *mashit tatties* and *bashid neeps* on the side, in other words mashed potatoes and whipped turnips. It was simple fare, but satisfied me.

Early that evening, the priest visited me as I lay in the attic recuperating from my surgery. I voiced my pleasure that he had returned, considering what I had told him during my confessional.

"Shh," he cautioned. "I have already told you that I am trained to hate the sin, but not the sinner. Now hush—we have company."

I saw he was accompanied both by Andrew and, to my surprise, Doctor Knox. The latter was dressed as garishly as before. I noticed that Andrew's clothes had been tailored along similar lines, except that they lacked the Doctor's frills and colour spectrum. The physician was a walking rainbow, whereas Andrew only wore black, white and grey, tones that suited his sober, morose nature.

"How are you feeling, sir?"

"Not too bad, Doctor Knox," I replied. "The discomfort has dwindled."

"Excellent. You still retain some recuperative powers." He glanced about the attic. "Andrew, you have told me the truth—this place is altogether inadequate for a man of his size." Turning back to me, he said, "I am going to relocate you to a basement room. Its proportions are better suited to your height and girth."

"Good," I said. "When may I move in?"

"Do you feel you are able to walk yet without too much discomfort?"

"Yes, I believe I can."

"In that case, Andrew will take you there directly."

On the way to the basement, I heard Doctor Knox say to Andrew, "More bodies must be harvested for organs. I will need them when I begin his next operations." He mentioned someone named Burke.

Walking was not difficult. Though the incision itched and twinged, it hurt less than before the operation. Andrew showed me into a modest, well-appointed chamber whose door opened onto a short hall that connected with the laboratory. The room contained two oak chests of drawers; a deep, wide mauve chair with arm-rests; a straight-back wooden seat with ornate etched figures on it, and a sturdy bed covered with a quantity of black woolen blankets. A carved mahogany night-stand beside it bore a chimney lamp and a small pile of books, uppermost of which was a Bible.

Andrew said that he would bring me the books from the attic, then bade me good-bye and closed the door. I settled onto the bed, which I found satisfyingly soft. Father Naman drew the straight chair close to me and sat, resting his stick against the wall. He wore his usual coarse cloak. In his hands he carried the large cowled robe that he'd had me don for the ride down from Pitlochry.

"This room is much more comfortable," I said. "Why didn't they put me here in the first place?"

"Because it is Andrew's bedroom."

"Doctor Knox made him give it up? That is wrong!"

"Calm yourself," he replied. "Napier volunteered to switch."

"But he can hardly bear to be near me!"

"Well, with you here and him in the attic, you still could not be farther apart."

"Father, we are the same distance away as before. Why would he do me such a favour?"

He thought it over. "For what it is worth, it is my impression that Knox represents the mind of this household, but Andrew Napier is its heart."

"Then what part of the body politic is Paterson the janitor?"

"That scamp?" A contemptuous snort. "He is its fundament."

I laughed at his unexpected earthiness.

Father Naman removed a letter from his robe and gave it to me. "Professor MacMorris received this today. It was forwarded from Pitlochry by the boy you borrowed your name from. Your pretend name, I mean."

I took the envelope and saw that though the front bore the Professor's name, the folded paper inside had been written to me.

TO MY ARCTIC RESCUER,

 I trust this finds you in better health. I hope you have remained firm in your resolve to do no further harm to any living soul.

 I have succeeded in selling my ship. Once the particulars of the sale are completed, I shall come to Pitlochry to visit with you and the MacMorrises.

 With compassionate regards,
 ROBERT WALTON

I penned a reply telling him that he must seek for us in Edinburgh. Father Naman promised to mail it for me the following morning, and then he picked up the long robe that he had brought and handed it to me. "I thought you might be feeling a bit cooped-up, and would wish to accompany me on a short walk. Doctor Knox says that if you feel up to it, he has no objections, though he does counsel caution."

"I am safe here," I argued. "Why would I wish to go out?"

"To visit the MacMorrises. They have been asking after you."

I immediately rose. "I should very much like to see them. Is it far?"

"Two short blocks, and a bit."

I expected the weather to be warm, but there was an unseasonal bite to the night air. I expressed surprise. Father Naman explained that the city was at the cross-roads of two cold fronts, that is what he called them: one that swept down from the Pentland hills north and west of town, the other a keen wind off the North Sea, which Leith, Edinburgh's maritime district, abuts.

"One of the local writers," he said, "characterizes Edinburgh's weather as 'treacherous,' and I would certainly agree to that."

Fortunately, we did not have very far to walk. A block of dormitory housing soon loomed up and I followed him inside. No students were in evidence; all was quiet. We climbed a flight of stairs and approached a door. The priest was about to knock, but suddenly we heard the sound of angry voices within. He paused. "Perhaps this is an inopportune time to visit."

"My friends are in danger!" Shoving myself in front of him, I pounded so hard that the lock broke, the door splintered and flew open.

"Was that really necessary?" the priest asked dolefully.

There were three people in the room—the Professor, Eve, and a boy perhaps her age or a bit younger. All three of them faced us, aghast.

"Who is that?" the Professor demanded, then, moving forward, saw, or rather guessed my identity from my size. "Will, is that you?"

"Yes."

"What did you do to the door?"

"I knocked too hard. I heard shouting, and thought you were in need of me."

"Willie, Willie," Eve laughed, "y'r ever my angel! But didna' y' learn at pool-side t' look before y' leap?"

"You know him?" The boy was shocked. He was tall with straw-hued hair and a set of muscles that suggested that he was no stranger to hard work.

"This is the friend that I wrote to you about, the one being treated by Doctor Knox. Will, this is my brother Hugh."

Father Naman and I exchanged a surprised glance. To the Professor, he said, "We did not know you have another child."

"He is *not* my son," he said frostily.

Eventually we sorted out what their argument was all about. Eve wanted to visit her mother, so she had prevailed upon Andrew Napier to write a message for her, one he promised and did send at once. The result was Hugh's unexpected (for the Professor) arrival. He meant to guide his sister to their mother's room in a part of town called West Port. That is what Eve's father objected to.

"West Port is a terrible neighbourhood!" he cried. "The lowest of the low!"

Hugh glared at him. "Mother and I live there. It is perfectly safe."

"Perhaps by day, but not at this hour!"

Eve argued that she had every right to go where she wanted, but the Professor reminded her that she was still a girl, and bound to obey him. Her reply was witheringly salty.

Well, they were at a total impasse. Venturing to intervene, I offered to be Eve's protector and accompany her and her brother on their journey (Hugh did not look pleased at the prospect). The Professor was anxious, but decided to agree. "Safety in numbers, I suppose, and size, as well. Very well, we will all go there, then—that is if you're willing, Father?"

"Yes," said the priest but, patting my arm, softly added, "Remember, Knox said to be cautious. Keep your face covered."

Hugh (I wondered what his last name was) guided us through a rough section called Grass-Market, and from there onto a twisted hill-side of old clothing shops and dingy lodging-houses; this, he said, was the West Port district. He took us to a street-loop called Tanner's Close, which curved round and back the way it started, and stopped in front of a sooty tenement.

"Here's where me and Mum live."

"Charming place," the Professor murmured ironically.

The boy glared. "It's good enough for t' likes o' us."

Whatever the Professor might have replied was cut short by the door suddenly opening with a shrill protest of rusty hinges. A burly brute with knotted hands and blunt fingers stood in the entry-way. "Well, lookie who's come t' pay us a visit! Professor MacD. an' cetra." The man next to him was a small ferret with sharp eyes that darted suspiciously. "Back from t' country, Professor, are ye?" the burly man inquired.

"Good evening, Burke," the Professor replied. "My daughter wants to see her mother. Is Patsy at home?" I wondered whether this was the Burke that I had heard mentioned by Doctor Knox.

"I think that she is busy, Professor," he answered. "Willie, fetch MacDougal, she'll know."

His companion turned round and shouted, "MacDougal, ye're wanted!"

"Willie, I could-a done that meself."

A grim woman appeared. "What's the damn shoutin' about?" Noticing the Professor, she immediately changed her tone. "Is it Patsy ye're wishin' t' see? She's tied up now, Professor." Burke and

Hare both sniggered at this. "Y' can wait for her, though, she won't be long. Show Daddy to y'r room, boy."

"He is not my father!" Hugh snapped. He took his sister's elbow. "This way."

They disappeared down the hall. At first the Professor made no move to follow, but must have decided his place was with his daughter, so he allowed the MacDougal woman to help him follow the pair.

I was wondering whether Father Naman and I should join the MacMorriss, when Burke, gawking in open-mouthed wonder, stepped up to me and whistled. "Ye mus' be seven feet tall!"

"Eight," I growled. "I do not like to talk about it."

"Burke, Burke, be ashamed o' yerself, man!"the ferret taunted. "First words out'n yer mouth, and ye've insulted 'im."

"I'll make it right, though, won't I, Will?"

That startled me. How did he know my pretended name? Then I realized that he was talking to his companion.

"C'm on," Burke said, "We'll stand ye t' a wee dram. Pub's round t' carn'r."

I was loath to go with this pair, but Father Naman murmured, "I think the MacMorriss *would* welcome a little privacy."

"But it's dangerous for me to be seen in public."

"A pub that this pair frequents ought not to be filled with folks of any worth or threat."

"Doctor Knox urged caution!"

"I will be beside you at all times."

Reluctantly, I agreed to the adventure.

The tavern was mercifully dark. Candles guttered precariously in pools of grease that affixed them to the wooden table-tops. Tobacco-smoke was thick enough to cut down visibility, but still heads turned and a buzz of talk sounded when I came in. I clutched my robe about my head so that there would be nothing to see but my eyes.

While Burke went to the bar, Hare—he introduced himself to me as we were walking—led us to a table big enough for four. Burke returned clutching foaming mugs; despite his promise of "a wee dram," he'd only spent enough for beer.

Father Naman raised his glass, but set it down again. "Will," he warned, "someone is sitting in that corner who I am surprised to see in a place like this."

I glanced that way and tried to be casual about it. A man dressed in garish colours saw me turn in his direction. He raised his pint at me in salute. His smile made me uneasy.

"Who is he?" I asked the priest.

"Deacon Brodie. I met him at St. Giles. I had not expected someone of his charactery in this place. Yet I have heard rumours about him."

"What sort of rumours?"

Burke, who had been listening, said, "That he follows in his father's foot-steps."

"Well," Hare observed, "'tis best not t' trust church-folk."

"Why," I asked, "does he look at me as if he knew who I am?"

None of them had an answer.

A meaty youth entered the pub. He was tall, but moved with an odd sort of lurch. Burke recognized him at once. "Ah, 'tis Daft Jamie! Call 'im over, Willie, we'll 'ave a bit o' fun."

Later, Andrew told me the boy's real name was James Wilson, but he was known to one and all as Daft Jamie. A sweet-natured, slow-witted youth of eighteen, who, in spite of his size, was often bullied by children half his age. All of the older folk were fond of him, though, as he ambled about town asking friends and strangers for "a wee dram," or a few spoons of tobacco to load up the silver snuff-box that he always carried with him.

Hare pushed a chair over to our table and asked Jamie to join us. The boy did so with touching eagerness. In his hand he held his silver snuff-box. Hare introduced him to me and Father Naman. Jamie's eyes were a warm, friendly brown, but his perpetually half-open mouth spoke of pitiable simplicity.

Burke brought him a pint of bitters, half of which Jamie swallowed in one gulp. Then, proceeding to what he called "a bit 'o fun," Burke laid his rough fist over the boy's snuff-box and said, "Now, Jamie, I've been patient wiv y', but ain't it time for y' t' return m' snuff-box, what y' borrowed over a month ago?"

Jamie set down his mug. "I never did!"

"Oh, yis, y' did," Hare chimed in. "Didn't I see it wiv m' own eyes? Y' told m' friend Burke y'd jist borr'a it till y' could get a new one fer yerself."

"This snuff-box belonged to m' Ma! I've nothin' else o' hers!" Tears began to well up in his eyes, but the ruffians laughed and called him a liar.

I'd had enough of this. I reached across the table, took Burke's hand in mine and tightened my fist. It took all the self-control that I have never had to stop short of shattering his bones.

"Let go," he gasped, face white as chalk, "and so will I."

I loosened my grip. Burke took his hand away from the snuff-box. I gave it back to Jamie. He stammered his thanks and swiftly quitted our table, though he took his pint with him.

With a ferocious curse, Burke shot to his feet and yanked the cloak away from my face. The pub was suddenly filled with screams.

Howling in anger, I leapt up and toppled both Burke and the table.

Someone was tugging at my arm; I nearly smashed him aside, but then realized that it was Father Naman.

I was horrified at myself. My old anger had reappeared!

"Let us get of here! *Now!*" the priest commanded.

We hurried back to the house where we had left Eve and her father.

"That was not good, what you did in there."

Trembling with unsuppressible rage, I said, "They meant to steal the one thing that reminds Jamie of his mother! I could not let that happen!"

"They were only teasing him. I grant you that he did not understand that, but they never would have really taken it away from him."

"How do you know that?"

"Everyone in Edinburgh likes Jamie. Had those rascals truly taken his snuff-box, they would have had half the town after them. All you did was make enemies of Burke and Hare."

I growled. "At least it was dark. Not many of them could have seen my face."

"But Deacon Brodie did."

A PRIVATE ARRANGEMENT

(?)

The problem admits of no easy answers. Ultimately, the beast deserves to die, but even if that end were easily achievable, which it is not, it is an undesirable option for reasons both complementary and contradictory.

While alive, he suffers. This is inarguable. If no other issue were raised, it alone would be ample justification for withholding the decisiveness of mortal retribution.

But, of course, there are other issues. The first, though not particularly vital, is an irritant. It is clear that in his quest to expiate his crimes, the beast has acquired friends, a new phenomenon in its life, and it provides an undeserved measure of solace. Closely allied to this is the thought that while his attempt at repentance may prove a misery to the creature, yet the attendant pains are somewhat assuaged—not only by the gentle trust of his new ersatz family, but the rugged grandeur of Scotland itself brings its own measure of consolation (at least that is somewhat mitigated by the city's dirt and decadence).

It might be possible to alienate him from his new friends, for it is unlikely that he would reveal to them the particulars of his evil past, yet their inherent goodness makes it by no means certain that they would abandon him if the truth were revealed. Yet even such an aim, if accomplished, would be insufficient. Resolution of a far more critical composition is necessary, yet it would be simplistic to wish for the *Sturm und Dräng* machinations that one encounters in the writings of Kyd, Shakespeare, or Graëbeck.

Two issues, then, must be recognized and satisfied; the first one is honour, a concept that, admittedly, I have generally regarded as empty, or at least artificial. Too often it is a masculine posturing whose dictates require bloodshed, and when one debates its distaff application it becomes mired in distasteful anatomical niceties. Yet despite the perhaps arguable truth of such declarations, honour still possesses a bed-rock denotation which can neither be ignored nor minimized.

The second issue is, to my mind, necessary for any society's survival. I refer to that social contract that distinguishes men from vicious animals. The thrust and force of government calls for laws to be drafted, approved and *enforced* to protect its citizenry from savage beasts in human guise; Edinburgh seems especially inflected with them.

The question, then, is how best to meet the requirements and demands of the cited institutions. I perceive various possibilities and mean to proceed in two distinct directions, hoping that, cumulatively, a resolution both proper and satisfying ultimately may be reached.

The man sat down across the table from me and smiled. There was nothing of good cheer or character in that spectacle.

"You have more resources than I realized," he observed.

"Does that mean, then, that you intend to provide me with certain assistances—? note that I employ a plural term."

He called for two pints of ale, but I told the waiter only to bring one. I would hire the man, if I could, but I would not drink with him. The mug was set down in front of him. He drank it in a single swallow, ordered another, and only then addressed me. "You speak of more than one thing that you want me to do. Will you pay me severally, or do you have a single fee in mind?"

"Have you a preference?"

"Yes." He sipped at his second ale. "Whichever arrangement profits me the most. Perhaps if you tell me your plan, we can assess a fair price."

That made me pause. I had not thought it all out, not every exigency; I suspected things must develop further before an ulltimate solution could be decided upon. I explained this to him.

"In that case," he replied, "let us proceed one step at a time. What is the first thing that you want me to do?"

I told him. He said how much I must pay him for it, I agreed, and money changed hands.

ǫoѕѕıpınǫ

(Andrew Napier)

It was Paterson's night off. I was in the basement when the bell to the alley rang and I opened the door and let in our patient. He bade good-night to the priest, who was off to St. Giles. The creature said, "Andrew, would you join me in my—your—room? I have a few things I would like to ask you."

I had no desire to comply, but telling him No would take more courage than I possess, so I followed him.

He settled in the armchair and waved me to sit on the straight-back. He thanked me for the books I had brought him, doing so with such child-like gratitude that I suddenly felt ashamed for constantly judging him for his appearance, which must ever be a source of grief for him.

"I met some people to-night," he told me. "Perhaps you know them."

"Tell me their names."

"First there is a boy called Daft Jamie."

"Everyone knows Jamie."

"When did his mother die?"

That made me sit up. "She's dead? I hadn't heard!"

He looked puzzled. "I guessed she is gone because he treasures this snuff-box that he carries, and says it is the only thing he owns that was hers."

"No, no, his mother is still alive. She threw him out into the street."

That angered him. "What?! Why would she treat her own son that way?"

"Jamie came home late one night, and his Ma had locked him out. But he's strong. He busted down the door, and looked for something to eat, but the lad is clumsy and he pulled down a cupboard full of his mother's dishes. When she came home and discovered the damage, out she tossed him. Ever since Jamie has lived off the mercy of his neighbours…well, the whole town, really. Everyone is fond of him."

"I am not so sure of that. There's a pair I met who treated him ill."

"Not towns-folk, surely?"

"Yes. One of them is named Burke, the other Hare."

"They are *not* towns-folk!" I complained. "They're Irish immigrants." I filled in some of their particulars for the patient, and did not neglect to mention Burke's mistress, Helen MacDougal, who manages a houseful of prostitutes.

"I met her tonight, as well," he said.

"Pretty company y've been keepin'."

"I did not get to meet Professor MacMorris's wife, though."

I waggled a finger. "They're not married. Not any longer."

"They are divorced?"

"Aye, and let me tell you, a divorce decree is a document that is next to impossible to obtain in this town. The sanctity of the family institution, don't y' know? But Professor MacMorris had strong grounds and nearly everybody's sympathy. This was back when Eve was a fairly tiny thing. Patsy Kensit … even when she was married she always used her maiden name. Now I ask y', what *is* the world coming to?! Anyway, Patsy was discovered carrying a child not of the Professor's fathering…which ought t' tell y' somethin' of their conjugal problems. So, as I say, he had grounds enough, and he got custody of Eve. He settled it so Patsy could afford to move out of his house, but the ensuing scandal, along with his slowly-fading eye-sight, prompted Professor MacMorris to move somewhere north where he reasoned there would be no prejudice against his daughter."

"Do you know who her brother Hugh's father is?"

"No-one knows that other than Patsy herself. Unless she's let her son in on the secret, but you would have to ask him that."

I did not voice my own suspicion of the boy's paternity, nor did I disclose the fact that Patsy Kensit is not just a lodger in Tanner's Close, but is one of the MacDougal's string of loose women.

I rose. "I hear the call of Doctor Knox's ledgers. I must return to work."

"Wait, Andrew, just one more question—who is Deacon Brodie?"

"Do y' mean the present Deacon, or his … well, infamous Daddy?"

"I did not meet the man, so I do not know if he is the father or the son."

"Oh, you saw the son. They hanged his father."

❧ ✿ ☙

There was not much Andrew could tell me about the present Deacon Brodie, other than Doctor Knox's dislike of him.

"Brodie," he said, "moves in the upper circles of society."

"That is surprising." I echoed Father Naman. "I saw him tonight in a dingy pub in West Port."

Andrew nodded with a grim smile. "That's Edinburgh, lad. Wherever y' go, you will come upon the high and the low rubbing shoulders."

Brodie's father, though, Andrew knew all about. The elder Deacon had been a wealthy cabinet maker, Deacon of the Incorporation of Wrights (a trade association), and a member of the town council. His profession enabled him to visit the homes of customers and fellow parishioners in the line of duty, but while there, he would secretly take wax impressions of their locks and keys, and have duplicates made so that his gang could burglarize the premises.

"He went on unsuspected for a goodly time," said Andrew. "but he made two errors. The first was attempting to rob the Scottish Excise Office. They caught his men, and one of them 'peached' on his chief in exchange for a pardon. Brodie fled to the Continent, but his second mistake was coming back too soon. He was recognized, arrested and—would you believe the irony?—sentenced to hang on a gallows of his own design. Even then, he almost defied justice. He devised a harness that he wore the day of his execution; he expected it to protect him from the shock of the fall. But it did not work. Folks claim that they heard his neck-bones snap a mile off!"

Andrew left me to ponder Deacon Brodie's fate. My sins were committed in open hostility, not devious subterfuge. To think that a successful man could lead two lives, one respectable, one evil … this upset me. But then my conscience smarted. What was the action of hiding little William Frankenstein's locket in the folds of Justine Moritz's dress but a strategem of the most repellent character?

I hated to admit it, but the elder Deacon Brodie and I were spiritually akin in duplicity.

THE FIRST MURDER

Next day, Paterson came rapping on my door and calling through it. "Doc wants y' richt na, dinna da'dle."

Soon, I was seated across the desk from Doctor Knox. Today he sported a burgundy coat over sleek black trousers. Another of what must be a series of diamond pins held his grey-striped cravat in place.

The Doctor appeared to be in good humour as he peered at me through spectacles instead of his usual eye-patch.

"The equipment I ordered has arrived," he said. "Tonight we begin our procedures in earnest."

"What kind of equipment did you get?" I asked. "You hinted at its being electrical in nature. Is it like what my creator used?"

He shook his head. "I daresay it is quite different from the devices he must have employed. Do you remember his laboratory?"

"Not as it was when I first opened my eyes. I was mute and distraught. Everything looked strange. I did not stay long. Afterward, though, I had occasion to watch as he attempted to duplicate his experiment."

"What?! He created life a *second* time?!"

"He did not finish," I replied bitterly. "His second laboratory was in the Orkneys. I watched his labours, as he sutured corpse-pieces together. He never got round to using the equipment—dials, knobs and wires entering into and radiating out of gear that I imagine would have channeled the lightning—the last thing he would have invoked to make her live. But then he betrayed me and destroyed the woman who was intended to be my mate."

"The memory upsets you. We need not talk of it further." He removed his spectacles and wiped them with a silk cloth. "I supposed something of the sort—the machinery he used to shock you alive. The principle is sound; you are its living proof. But the operations that begin to-night depend upon a subtler form of electrical manipulation."

I sought details.

"Tonight," he said, at ten p.m., I'll show you the instruments that I ordered and explain their purpose before we begin."

Promptly at ten I opened the door and stepped along the short corridor leading to the laboratory. Doctor Knox was there, and so was Paterson, but except for a three-panel folding screen in a far corner, I saw nothing in the way of new equipment. I thought the screen had been set up as a protective shield for the Doctor to step behind as he worked whatever electrical gadgets he meant to use.

As I walked in, Paterson's grizzled face registered his usual displeasure. His eyes squinted, his forehead puckered, his mouth turned down as if some noxious odour assailed him. He jerked a thumb at the operating table. "Get on't," he ordered, "so's I c'n strap y' doon."

"Not yet," the Doctor contradicted. "I need to talk to the patient. Leave us alone. I will call you back when I need you."

"Richt." The janitor left, though I didn't watch him go because my attention was riveted by a tray that Doctor Knox picked up and brought close. On it was a large assortment of long needles with sharp points.

"What are those?"

"The equipment that I have been waiting for."

"What are you going to do with those?"

"What does it look like?"

I controlled my temper with the usual difficulty. "Doctor, I accept the unpleasant fact that you must cut into me with nothing to dull the pain. But do you think I will also permit you to turn me into a living pin-cushion?"

"Be patient and listen. I think you will change your mind."

"There is no harm in listening," I conceded.

"Excellent." He set the needles to one side. "Shortly after I graduated from Edinburgh University, I served as an assistant surgeon in a military hospital in Belgium, and after that sailed with my regiment to South Africa. It was there that I met a Doctor named Usui. Early in his career, he had left his country determined to travel the world. In Africa, he perceived that the villagers relied on shamans whose healing depended more on magic than folk remedies. He decided to treat those willing to accept his help. He used an ancient technique practiced for thousands of years in China, virtually unknown in the

West. I learned what I could about his system, though to become truly adept in it takes long years of practice.

"The needles help control, modify and rechannel the body's natural electro-chemical currents. I submitted to such treatment myself and I promise you that the insertion of the needles does not hurt. Quite to the contrary, I passed into an altered state of consciousness that is simultaneously exhilarating and relaxing. Doctor Usui said that with proper needle placement, he could perform practically painless surgery, but I admit that I am not sufficiently adept to achieve that."

He was suddenly interrupted by the clanging of the alley-door bell.

"Paterson," he called, "come down and get the door." He waited, but when the janitor did not answer, he cursed mildy and opened the door himself.

I saw him stiffen. He bent down to inspect something that I could not see. Then he stood up and, venting a much stronger imprecation, shouted for Paterson.

Paterson clattered down the stairs. Doctor Knox strode across the room and blocked him from entering. "Fetch Andrew. Wake him up, if necessary, then go home."

Paterson began to utter thanks, but the Doctor cut him off. "Andrew—*at once!*"

As Paterson bounded up the stairs, Doctor Knox turned to me and said, "I have to postpone your surgery till tomorrow night. Do you mind going to your room?"

"If I must."

"You have my gratitude."

As I entered my bed-chamber, I passed Andrew hurrying into the laboratory clad in pyjamas and a tattered grey night-gown. I left my door cracked, and stood behind it, listening.

"What's wrong?" Andrew asked.

"There's a body outside."

"I'll fetch it."

"Wait. You are going to recognize him. It is the lad that they call Daft Jamie."

With a roar, I drove my fist into the wall, dislodging a quantity of plaster.

Doctor Knox pushed open my door. "Well, you have obviously heard. In that case, would you mind helping us? Jamie's rather big for

Andrew to manage."

I forced myself to unclench my fists and went to the alley-door. They had put the boy in a burlap sack. I picked him up and set him gently onto the operating table.

Doctor Knox bent over the corpse and investigated. "Suffocated," he declared. "The last body Burke brought us looked much the same as this."

"Burke wouldn't *dare!*" Andrew protested. "Not Daft Jamie!"

"Perhaps not. But more to the point, Burke would not leave us a present. He would wait for his fee."

"Then who could have done it, Doctor? Why would anyone kill Jamie?"

"Andrew, that is not our concern. The question is what do we do about it."

"Should I report this to the authorities?"

Doctor Knox turned red. "Andrew, are you mad? You want to give my enemies a reason to shut us down—for they will, you know!"

"What do we do, instead?"

"There is no point in harvesting his organs. Tobacco and alcohol have surely rendered them past all reclamation. We will just have to use him as a teaching tool."

"But the students would recognize him at once!"

"Not if you cut off his head." Doctor Knox turned to me. "May I count on you to keep our secret?"

"What if I do not?"

"Then you are no longer my patient." And with that, he left the room.

THE PASSION OF FRANKENSTEIN

June 23rd—Midsummer's Eve.

I learned that fact when, upon hearing an odd sound, I opened my door and saw Paterson perched upon a step-stool nailing a sprig of mistletoe to the lintel.

"What is that for?" I asked. "I thought that was only put up at Christmas."

"Na'," the janitor answered. "It goes up t' Eve o' St. George's Day, and t'marra is t' feast o' John-Baptist, an' that means t'nicht's Midsoomer's Eve, so y' know what t'at means."

"No, I don't. Tell me."

"T' nicht before a Saint-day, all t' evil sperrets will be a-walkin'. T' mistletoe keeps 'em off 'n' awa'." He got down from the stool and took it into the laboratory. I supposed he was going to nail another sprig to the alley-entry.

I thanked his retreating back for the favour, not that he gave any sign that he had heard me, but I thought it was proper to express my gratitude, not because I am the least bit superstitious, but Paterson's action seemed to be the first friendly thing he had ever done on my behalf. Then it occurred to me that he probably thought of me as one of the evil spirits he was warding off.

I had not seen Eve or the Professor since the night that I went with them to West Port, and Father Naman had taken on some clerical duties at St. Giles in exchange for the continued use of the pallet there on which he slept. Thus his companionship, which I had come to rely upon, was necessarily curtailed.

I was beginning to feel like a prisoner. During the day, I never left my room. The time hung heavy on my hands. I read a lot, of course, and Andrew brought me a book of "solitaire" games one could play with a deck of cards, which he also furnished. The gesture pleased me, though the oblong paste-boards proved too difficult for my clumsy hands to handle. Still, as trepidatious as Andrew was when he was near me, he seemed to feel some sympathy for my enforced isolation.

A soft tap. I opened the door, expecting Paterson to be on the other side, but was glad to see Andrew, instead. "I hope I am not disturbing you?" he asked in his usual diffident fashion.

"Come in," I said. "Don't hover in the arch-way—it is your room, after all."

"I knocked because though it is only a little after eight o'clock, Doctor Knox says that he would like to get started a little earlier this evening."

"So he does mean to operate on me to-night?"

"Yes, and it will be a major procedure. He wants to find out whether the knife wound you sustained caused damage to your liver or stomach or lungs. Or all of them—and he may also inspect the upper loops of your intestines and your spleen. I think that he is really chiefly concerned with the liver, though, for that would wreak the most havoc over time."

I thanked him for his explanation. It was a fuller account of what Knox planned to do than anything the Doctor had ever bothered to impart to me.

"Ah, well," said Andrew, fidgeting nervously with his fingers, "he does not mean to keep y' in t' dark, it is just his way. A genius prefers his own counsel."

That I understood. Knox shared that characteristic, at least, with Victor Frankenstein. "And yet, Andrew, he did take the time to tell you his plans. I appreciate you passing along the information to me."

That made him smile, a charming transfiguration. "He never shares things with me. I flatter myself that I represent to Doctor K. an imperfect, but reasonably useful tool. A *confidant*? Never, not even when I was one of his students."

"I did not know that you were. So what you have told me is your own idea of what he intends to do to-night?"

"Yes. He is also going to do I-don't-know-what with those Chinese needles. But I would trust him as to their purpose and use."

That made me suspicious. "Did he order you to reconcile the patient with his instruments of Oriental torture?"

Andrew went white. "Doctor K. only told me to ready you for surgery. He has no idea I would tell you anything else…so please do not mention it to him!"

"Very well. I believe you."

Suddenly I felt weary and, in spite of myself, angry. No matter what Doctor Knox and his assistant believed to be true, I knew with righteous certainty that Burke and Hare were responsible for Daft Jamie's murder, and it was all that I could do to stop myself from rushing over to Tanner's Close and break their necks. I hated the silence that the Doctor required me to maintain, for it were judged by legal authorities, it would make me what they call an accomplice after the fact.

These thoughts had turned my attention inward. When I re-focused, I was surprised to see Andrew still standing in the door-way.

"Yes," I said brusquely, "I know. Tell the Doctor that I will be there soon."

Putting a finger to his lips, Andrew produced a paper sack from behind his back and, handing it to me, departed.

I opened the bag. Within it I found two quart bottles of scotch whisky. Silently thanking Andrew, I downed them both and hid the empties.

It was not easy to walk the short distance from my room to the laboratory. I set my feet down very slowly and carefully. The room was as before. Other than the folding screen in the corner, the room was sparely appurtenanced: the operating table with its leather straps was in the center, and near it were a few side tables that held a variety of surgical gear and, on one of them, Doctor Knox's Asian needles.

I lay down on the operating table and Andrew began to strap me down. When he was done and had looked away, I flexed the muscles of my arms and legs. The straps were thick and strong, but if—when!—the pain proved more than I could deal with, I thought it probable that I could snap my restraints.

Not that I mean to do so…*I am determined to suffer penance!* Yet I did not wholly trust myself. All too often, I had proved unable to control the blind rages that seize me. It *will* hurt, I told myself—and you *deserve it!*

I silently recited the litany of my sins:

Elizabeth Lavenza (*Forgiven!*)—

Henry Clerval (*Forgiven!*)—

William—little William (*Forgiven!*)—

Baron Frankenstein (*Not my fault!*)—

Victor Frankenstein—but despite what Father Naman had counseled, I could not altogether absolve myself from the horrors that I visited upon my creator.

Justine Moritz—

Mea culpa!

The needles did not hurt. I was pleased to learn that they were instrumental in rendering me extremely relaxed, an effect that surely built upon the great quantity of whisky I had imbibed.

But when Doctor Knox's monogrammed scalpel began to cut into my abdomen, nothing abridged the pain. I screamed and screamed. All consciousness was suddenly transformed into endless agony. I howled and thrashed, but the straps held. Thought became impossible. I could not think of penance or of anything. I was incoherent. The gradations and variations of torment blocked out everything but pure bestial anger and fear.

Get free!

Kill!

KILL!

A gentle stroke upon my hand, another across my forehead...and my pain began to die away. I still hurt, but the level was suddenly manageable. I could think again. I looked up into eyes brimful of tears that fell upon my wounds like droplets of Heaven's soft rain.

"I was wrong!" Father Naman cried. "No-one deserves to suffer this much!"

A Favour for a Friend

Sleep seldom comes easily, but as Doctor Knox removed the Asian needles, an activity which I found oddly fascinating to watch, my eye-lids began to grow heavy. I closed them for what I thought would only be a moment, but then I passed into a state of reverie that was rife with incident. Victor Frankenstein was in my dreams once more, but unlike the nightmare I had in Pitlochry forest, this time he looked upon me with a compassion that he had never shown me when he was alive.

When at last I woke up, it was late afternoon of the next day. Somehow, they had managed to put me to bed in Andrew's room. I lay there for a long time gazing listlessly at the ceiling. Gradually I became aware that I was not alone. For some time, I realized, I had been hearing a long, sustained whispering, so I rolled onto my side, not without a severe twinge of pain, and saw that Father Naman was sitting close to me. His eyes were shut, but he was not asleep, for I could see that his lips were shaping words that I could not hear, so I gathered that he must be at his prayers.

As I thought that, I heard him say, "Amen," and then he opened his eyes and returned my gaze. "I thought that I had heard you stirring. Does it hurt much?"

"Yes, but it is bearable if I do not move."

Fate must have heard; no sooner had I spoken, when there was a tap on my door, and it opened to reveal Professor MacMorris. A medical student had guided him from the dormitory where he was staying.

"Will," he said, "I came to ask you a favour."

(Father Naman)

MacMorris had not encountered Doctor Knox or Andrew on his way in, so he did not know that his friend had just undergone surgery. Before I could tell him, he revealed his problem—his daughter had decided to stay with her mother and brother in Tanner's Close. I tried to reason with him. "They are, after all, her family, too. It is only natural that she would want to stay and get to know them."

"Father Naman," he replied, "are you aware of what goes on in that house?"

"Y-e-es…" A jerk of my head to convey the thought that it would be better not to let *him* know, but I should have realized that MacMorris would not see my gesture.

"The MacDougal," he said, "manages prostitutes there. My former wife is one of them. That is why I do not want my daughter anywhere near them!"

The creature got out of bed, but the effort cost him dearly; he cried out.

"Will," MacMorris exclaimed, "what is the matter with you?"

I told him that he had surgery the preceding night.

"Och, I am so sorry, lad! Get back in bed! I should not have come!"

But the damage was done. "Will" insisted on going to West Port at once. I argued with him that he was too weak for such a protracted walk, but he shouted for Andrew. Doctor Knox appeared, instead.

"Why is the patient out of bed?" he demanded.

"My friend," said the creature, "needs me to go to West Port."

"Have you lost your senses?" Knox barked. "Do you want to rip open your sutures?"

"This is all my fault," said MacMorris, "Will, please get back in bed!"

"You need my help!"

"Attempt to leave," Knox warned, "and I will sedate you so that you will not wake up for weeks."

The creature took one step that brought him close to the Doctor. "You will observe that I am not strapped to your table."

A tense silence, and then Knox did something unexpected …he smiled.

"Very well," he said, deigning to look up—far up—to make eye contact, "it is your body. If you want to risk it, I will freely admit that you have the right to do so. But since I have expended so much effort on your behalf—unremunerated effort, mind you—allow me, at least, to strap your wounds—not *those* straps!—only a heavy swath of bandage to prevent massive bleeding."

"That would be a good thing," the patient admitted.

I admit that I was being head-strong and foolish, but in all my miserable life, I had never before had friends, but now that I had three—(for all his compassion, I did not count Captain Walton one of them)—I would give my life to protect them.

The priest kept his wits about him. After I had been bandaged so tight by the Doctor that I could scarcely breathe, Father Naman suggested that we take the Professor back to his lodging. Token resistance was made, but I think that the Professor was relieved not to have to accompany us. We promised him that we would bring Eve back safely.

Once he was again ensconced in his dormitory (I was glad to see that the front door had been repaired), Father Naman and I walked slowly toward the West Port district. Even with the tight bandages, every step was agony. I was surprised at how depleted were my stores of energy. I had never felt so weak.

When we had almost reached our destination, my companion told me to stop for a moment and listen to him. "The last thing that we must do," the priest warned me, "is to call attention to ourselves."

"I agree, Father."

"Good. But there are some things that I must tell you. First, the night that Burke tore the cloak away from your face—people have been talking about it all over town."

"But not many could have seen me!"

"It only takes a few persons to start a rumour."

"Well, nobody knows where I am, though …do they?"

"During the last operation, your screams were heard. An angry buzz has been stirred up, though so far it is only directed at Doctor Knox. But if word gets out that the giant in West Port is his screaming patient, you may be sure that there will be trouble." With a wince of pain, he rested his weight upon his stick. "The second thing which you need to know is that there is talk going round concerning Henry Clerval's murder."

I laboured to breathe. "What is being said?"

"That his murderer is somewhere in Edinburgh."

"How could anyone know *that*!? It happened so far off!"

"I have no idea. So I must stress emphatically that you must be very, very careful." He rested a hand on my wrist. I felt his calming warmth and power. "When we arrive at Burke's house, please stay in the shadows. I will only call on you if it is absolutely necessary."

"You are afraid that I may do violence to myself?"

"I am more concerned about what you might do to Burke or MacDougal."

(Father Naman)

He agreed to wait outside. I told him that if our mission met resistance, his being close at hand ought to prove effective. Agreeing, he crossed Tanner's Close to stand beneath an awning where the streetlamp's glow did not reach.

I knocked. Burke opened the door. I told him why I was there. He laughed at me and shut the door in my face. I knocked again. No answer.

I knocked again, and kept on knocking till at length the noise fetched him back.

"Father," he said, "I mean y' no disrespect, but this ain't any of y'r business, so kindly be off with y'."

Before he could shut the door again, I asked him to oblige me by looking across the Close at the door to Number Seventeen.

Burke did so. As he did, the creature took a step out of the shadows.

"Tell me, " I asked, "would you rather deal with him?"

Cursing, the rascal allowed me to enter.

The weather was mild, and nobody stirred. I leaned against the wall; it eased the pain of my wounds.

Time passed. I was almost asleep on my feet when furtive noises across the way roused me. I saw a pair of figures huddled together. I recognized both of them. One was Burke's friend Willie Hare, which was no surprise since the ferret lived there, too. But the other man was Paterson, Doctor Knox's janitor. What was *he* doing in Tanner's Close?

Something too small for me to see exchanged hands. Had this transaction happened in the alley abutting Doctor Knox's basement laboratory, I suppose that it would signify that Hare was receiving payment for delivering a corpse. But whatever the thing was that was handed off, it was traveling in the wrong direction, for Hare was passing it to Paterson.

The front door opened. Hare shoved Paterson away; the janitor swiftly quitted the place as Father Naman emerged carrying Eve in his arms. It was a deal of a burden for him.

"Where, Fath'r," Hare demanded, "d'y t'ink y'r goin' wiv 'er?"

"I'm taking her back to her father."

"And does t' MacDougal know t'is so?"

The priest did not reply. He began crossing the Close to me.

"Y'r stealin' prime merchandise!" Hare shouted. "MacDougal! C'm oot!"

I stepped forward so that the villain could see me.

"Ne'er mind!" Hare shouted, quickly entering the house and shutting the door.

Eve was fast asleep. She did not wake, not even when we brought her to the dormitory and Professor MacMorris put her to bed.

SKULDUGGERY

(Hugh Kensit)

I can not say why exactly, but there is something wrong. Something bad. I have always trusted what you can see, measure and add up more than I have the power of intuition, but you can not live in this town without experiencing an occasional chilly sensation along your spine, and this was definitely one of those times. I did not know where to look, who or what to ask, or where to go, which just added to my nervousness, a condition that I am not usually subject to, and that just made things worse.

(Helen MacDougal)

Patsy shambled into the room and collapsed on the old quilt in the corner. She was shivering, but not from the cold. With her teeth chattering, she said, "I canna work t'night less'n—" but then a sudden spasm shook her like a rag-doll. I knew just what she needed.

"Dinna fear," I told her. "I've got a favour t' ask y', and once it's done, you know that I will take care of y', Patsy."

She moaned. "Canna work, canna do nothin', do ye no' see that?"

Of course she was right, I could see that sure enough, but I had to keep her on edge. "A wee dose, Patsy, that is all y'r gonna git f'r now. Plenty more, though, when y' do me m' favour."

"Wee dose!" she muttered. "*MacDougal, please!* Fix me oop proper!"

So I told her what she had to do. In the state she was in, she would have agreed to worse.

All this, though, was before the priest forced his way in.

Later that night, I was about to go to bed when Burke burst into the room, and shouted, "What's been goin' on, bitch?" He hauled off and slapped me.

I slapped him right back, and harder. "Do that again and it's m' knee ye'll be feelin' y' know where!"

In spite of himself, he smiled. "Y'r a guid lass, MacD. Now come wi' me."

I followed him. When we got there, Hare was already waiting for us.

I glared at the pair. "How did y'have the nerve to go and do this without askin' me first?"

"Stow it!" Hare said. "What are we gonna do?"

"What's the problem, gents? Trundle the barrow over t' Surgeon's Square."

Burke shook his head. "Wisht we could. But we can't." He pointed a finger at me. "Stay here with Willie. One of y' keep watch outside, t'other keep this door shut."

"Where are *you* goin'?"

"T' find th' Deacon."

(Deacon Brodie)

This was not part of the plan. It was completely unexpected, and I did not like it. Still, hard cash is a powerful argument, so I went to the pub and was about to fee me a messenger to fetch Burke, when who should turn up and save me the cost of a pint?

"Sit thee doon, Burke," I told him. "I know why you are here."

That surprised him. "Are y' spyin' on us, then?"

"And what if I am?" I dropped a large handful of coins on the table. "Now that is half of what ye'll earn if y' get this done fast."

Burke lit up a pipe and puffed it. "It's not enough for the risks involved."

"Y' don't even know yet what I'll be telling y'."

"That don't matter none." A puff of smoke. "That is enough coin fer me, but there is also Willie and MacDougal t' square."

"So they all know?"

A nod and another gust of smoke. There was nothing for it but to set down more cash.

Burke leaned forward. "*Now* I'll hear yer plan … "

(?)

In the distance I heard a sad lament. It was the old blind lady who sang for coin in front of St. Bernard's Parish House. I waited impatiently in a shadowy corner; it was a long vigil, but at last I heard the unsteady clatter of a cart on the cobble-stones and, risking a glance, saw their approach.

"Is it here, then?" Hare asked.

"Aye," Burke answered. "Deacon said t' find a dark part o' th' street, an' not t' linger."

"And why would we want to do that?"

"Aren't y' t' least bit curious, Willie?"

"Not enough t' risk m' neck."

While they were talking, I could hear them grunting with the effort of emptying the cart.

"Well, that's that. Let us splurge on a wee dram, Willie."

"If'n y'r buyin', Burke."

The cart rattled and rumbled as they wheeled it back the way they came. I did not trust them, though, so I waited a long time after their noise dwindled in the distance before emerging.

The last distasteful thing that had to be done did not take long.

As I stood up, I suddenly realized it was much too silent.

When had the blind woman stopped singing?

THE BLIND WOMAN'S SONG

(Lizzie Bowers)

I was working late that night at the clinic and so I turned the key in the lock as quietly as I could, and took off my shoes before entering so that I would not wake up my sister.

To my surprise, Connie was sitting by the open window, wide awake. "Lizzie," she asked me, "would y' mind brewin' up a pot o' tea?"

"O' course not. But I'm surprised y'r not fast asleep, Connie."

"Well, I tried to, but … "

"But what?"

She shook her head. "I'm sure it is nothing."

"What is nothing, Connie?"

"Tea, *please*?"

"All right." I hung up my shawl and nurse's cap and went to the kitchen and brewed a hearty pot of gun-powder tea, which I laced with a few thimbles of brandy.

A nippy breeze tingled my skin as I returned to the front room. "Connie, why did y' open the window?"

My sister shivered. "Now y' mention it, it is a trifle chilly. I'll shut it." She did so. "I was listening to old Jenna singing across the way at St. Bernard's."

I handed her a mug of tea and sat down beside her and we both sipped contemplatively for a time.

"Have you ever spoken to Jenna?" I asked.

"Never have, Lizzie. Why do y' ask?"

"I have always had the feeling that the woman is a fraud. I think she can see perfectly well."

"*Really*? I never would have thought it!"

That was one of my sister's most endearing traits, and I loved her for it.

"But, Lizzie … " She hesitated.

"Yes?"

"I think you may be right, perhaps Jenna can see."

"Why do you say that?"

Connie sipped tea and stared out the window for a moment before she replied. "Well, there is something that happened earlier. It is what kept me awake, wondering."

"Tell me."

"Jenna was singing this beautiful song, it was ever so stirring. *Men of Harlach*, do y' know it?"

I nodded. "It's Welsh, which figures because that is where Jenna comes from."

"I did not know that!"

Well, how could she, after all? Connie sat by the window for hours so she could hear the sounds of life passing her by. She had lost the use of her legs when she was a little girl.

"All right, Connie. Jenna was singing, y' said, and then what?"

"She stopped."

"You mean, she'd finished the song?"

"No, she cut it off right in the middle! I have never known her t' do that before!"

"Did something interrupt her?"

Connie nodded decisively. "There was a rumble that got louder, and then it stopped. I looked out the window and saw these two men pushing some kind of cart and moving toward Jenna. That is why I think maybe she *saw* them."

"Why do y' think that?"

"Because I heard her say, 'Willie, how are y', an' who's y'r friend?' "

CALM BEFORE THE STORM

The weather turned oppressively hot. Andrew said the warm wind was attracting clusters of midges, tiny gad-flies that brought misery to both man and beast, though I was not troubled by them, for I stayed in my room, feeling altogether spent.

Father Naman had work to do at St. Giles, and Andrew's brief visit was mainly for the purpose of bringing me my breakfast and to see whether I had sustained any damage during my visit to West Port. Finding I was no worse than very tired, he left me. I ate, then got back in bed and slept till late morning.

A rap at the door woke me, and Doctor Knox himself entered. It was a no-patch day. Adjusting his spectacles, he studied me with interest.

"I wanted to see for myself if you are all right." He palpated and peered at the sutures for a few moments, then nodded. "Andrew was correct. Your wounds are closed, including the knife-gash, and your leg-bone is finally beginning to knit. Otherwise, how are you feeling?"

"If I stay in one spot, there is no pain."

"Excellent," he said. "I am sure that you will not repeat last night's folly."

As he started out the door, I could not help but sigh. He stopped.

"What is troubling you?"

"Doctor, I am just bored."

"Didn't Andrew provide you with reading matter?"

"He did. He also brought me playing cards, and he is trying to teach me how to play draughts, but the cards and chequers are too small for me to handle well."

Stroking his chin, he looked thoughtful. "I will tell you what," he said, after a moment. "Except for one autopsy lecture—an old woman died outside St. Bernard's—otherwise my schedule today is uncommonly free. The anatomy class will take me about an hour. Come to my office after that and I will show you a new game that you ought to be able to manipulate."

I rose from bed. Movement still hurt.

"Take your time, I won't be there for an hour," he said. "Come down, then, and I will be waiting for you."

When I got there, the Doctor had cleared off the top of his desk and set an object, or rather, a series of objects upon it that I recognized from pictures in books, though this was the first time that I had ever seen one: a huge chess-board with all of the playing pieces arranged upon it. The design of the chess-men was of a Medieval army. Each piece was big enough for me to grasp without dropping it, nor disturb its neighbours on the adjacent squares.

Doctor Knox embarked upon an explanation of the history and rules of the game. I listened, altogether fascinated. Here was a thing as inessential as my existence, yet it had both point and purpose. To master it must be a joyful thing, and I said so.

"Indeed," the Doctor agreed. "It takes time and perseverance, and demands a mind able to plan strategy many moves in advance. Chess is very old, yet it is not alone in dating back to antiquity. It is one of several classic games that reflect core values of those cultures that gave rise to each. The Romans produced backgammon, in which every man has an equal chance to race ahead and win. The Asian game Go, on the other hand, permits one to call upon an infinite number of playing pieces, calling to mind the huge populations of the East. Chess, though, mirrors India's rigid caste system. Each man has a defined function, and only the lowly pawn has a remote chance to better its powers." He smiled, though not with cameraderie. His expression was wintry. "I have not taught you this game merely to alleviate your ennui. I want to know the potency and limitations of the mind that you received from Victor Frankenstein."

In turn, I gave him my own wintry smile. "So you know more about me than I have revealed. I rather suspected that you do."

"The Henry Clerval murder," he said, "drew considerable attention, even this far away from where it took place."

"Yes, but—"

He waved away whatever I was about to say. "Your secret is safe with me. The physician and the priest are both constrained by oaths of confidentiality."

Despite the alarum clattering in my mind, I decided to accept what he was and was not telling me. "Tell me more about your decision to teach me chess."

That produced a smile closer to genuine. "Chess, for all its remarkable history and glamour, appeals only to the new player and the experienced. Most who take it up give it up. Perhaps you are one of the few who will pass on to the game's higher levels."

With that declaration, Doctor Knox began to play chess with me.

Predictably, he won the first games swiftly, but by the fifth game, he had to work harder. He still won. But the sixth game ended in a tie. Rising, Doctor Knox said, "That, sir, deserves a toast." He went to a side-board and fetched two tumblers and a bottle of scotch.

"But I did not win," I protested, "I only tied you."

He poured, handed me a glass and clinked his against mine. "Dear patient," he declared, "it is no small feat for a new player to tie an experienced one. To your health!"

We drank together; at the first taste, my eyes widened in appreciation. This scotch was ever so much better than what I had been served in the laboratory, and I said so.

"Indeed it is," he nodded. "It was aged for twenty-five years in a sherry cask, hence its sweetness. But you will also note an astringency in the after-taste; that is because it was distilled along the coast-line of one of the western isles. Sea-water, which contains iodine, infuses the whisky as it matures." As he spoke, he busied himself at the chess-board, removing some pieces and rearranging others. When he was done, he asked me to look at the position that he had created. "I have set you what is called an endgame problem. Imagine that you are the white player. You must play so that you achieve checkmate within four moves."

"Must I do so mentally, or may I move the pieces?"

"Whichever works for you. If you fail, return to this pattern and try it again."

It was no easy task. I made several mistakes, but by the fourth attempt I accomplished my task.

Doctor Knox poured me another tumbler of scotch. "Now do not let this make your brain go fuzzy," he said, resetting the chess pieces into a new arrangement. "This time you are black, and you must checkmate white in three moves."

In such fashion, the morning slipped into early afternoon. The sultry weather turned dark; the Doctor looked out the window and, seeing a great storm was brewing. "I must leave you now," he said. "I have a task to perform at the hospital, and I had best be on my way before the rain comes." As he rose to put away the scotch and wipe the tumblers, I asked him whether he would let me take the chess-board and pieces to my room to practice.

"I have another set up-stairs, it is not quite as large as this one, but I believe it is still big enough for you to handle. I will get it when I return and have Andrew bring it down to you." A sly smile. "I will set you a new endgame problem that you may work upon in your room. No one I have shown it to has ever solved it."

"Show me now!"

He selected five chess-men and put them on the board with the black rook in the upper-left corner and the black king one square beneath. On the second row from the upper left, he put a white pawn one square to the right of the black king and the white rook one square to the right of the white pawn. Finally, he placed the white king two squares directly below the white pawn.

This, then, was the position—

"You are white," Doctor Knox said, "and must effect checkmate in one move."

"*One move?*" I echoed. "Surely that cannot be difficult!"

"No? Study the board."

I did so for several minutes. There was no move I could make with the white king that would bring about a checkmate, for kings are not permitted to take a square adjacent to one another. Anywhere else I might place the white king would not endanger the black king.

The same thing was true of the white rook, the difference being that he could not move to the top row or the black rook would capture him.

So my only remaining option would be to advance the white pawn to the top row where he could be exchanged for another piece—but even if I promoted him to become a white rook, bishop or queen, either the black rook or the king would instantly capture him.

"It is not possible," I declared at last.

"Yes, it is. But in order to solve my puzzle, you must learn to—" He suddenly stopped. For the last few moments, we had become aware of a raucous grumble of voices outside that had been growing louder as it drew nearer. "Andrew!" the Doctor called. That worthy shortly appeared.

"Yes, sir?"

"Go and find out what is causing that infernal racket outside."

Andrew left the room. He returned, pale and shaken.

"Well?" Doctor Knox demanded.

"There is a mob at the door."

"What do they want?"

Andrew, cringing, pointed at me. "Him."

THE SECOND MURDER

Thunder rumbled in the distance. Doctor Knox told me not to show myself unless he instructed me to do so, then he opened the door and, facing the crowd, demanded to know why they were disturbing the peace. Angry shouts and imprecations...but I recognized one voice that stood out over the rest of the crowd. It was Hugh, Eve's brother.

"Bring out your beast!" he shouted.

A flicker of distant lightning. "I have no idea what you are talking about," the Doctor replied.

"I am talking about your patient," Hugh cried. "The monster who came to my house and murdered my mother!"

The Doctor stiffened. "Patsy is dead?"

"They found her in a close off Lawn-Market."

"Why do you think my patient would kill her?"

"So you can have more organs for your diabolical operations!" His assertion produced threatening sounds of assent from the crowd.

"Strange," Doctor Knox "I have had no such deliveries. When did this murder take place?"

"Last night, or early this morning."

Turning to me, the Doctor murmured, "Tell me that you did not do this thing when you went there against my advice."

"I never even entered the house."

"In that case, it is time that you met your accusers." He stood to one side and beckoned me to step forward.

When the crowd saw me, anger gave way to fear. Some of them gasped, some shrieked; most shrank back, though not Hugh.

"This is my patient. He has not set foot outside these walls," Doctor Knox lied. "If you are determined to take him, note his size. Imagine his strength." To me he whispered, "Do nothing unless they attack. But if they do, I will be your witness that what you did was in self-defense."

I took a step towards them.

A long silence. No one moved a muscle.

I took another step.

A sudden crack of lightning. My thoughts raced with vivid images of the justifiable destruction I would wreak if they moved against me—and how I yearned for them to do so!

But at my third step, the crowd broke and ran. I felt relieved but also—I am ashamed to admit it—disappointed.

Hugh alone remained. Doctor Knox told him to come inside.

We were back in the Doctor's office. I said to Hugh, "Your father and sister have been extremely kind to me. They are my dear friends. I would never hurt them, or their family."

The youth put a hand to his eyes. "I believe you."

"Good," Doctor Knox said. "Now I need details, lad. How was Patsy killed?"

Hugh glared. "Of course, I should have expected you to show such ghoulish interest!"

I thought the Doctor was going to slap him. But he controlled his anger, clutching the back of a chair tightly. "Young man," he said, "Once I knew your mother. We were friends."

Looking from one to the other, a thought suddenly struck me, though I did not voice it.

"I think she was strangled," Hugh said.

"Think? You are not sure?"

"Burke made me go to the police. I identified her, but I could not bear to look long."

The Doctor nodded. "Stay here, the two of you, I will see what I can find out from the police." He put on his hat and top-coat, found an umbrella and left us to wait in his office.

We did so for a long, long, long time. Finally I spoke. I asked whether Eve knew her mother was dead.

"No, I do not not think that she does." We endured another lengthy interval, and then he said, "I suppose it is up to me to tell her."

"If you wish me to, I will tell her father."

That suggestion did not sit well with him, but when at length he responded, it was with sadness, not anger. "It is my responsibility. I will do it. Though first, I would like to hear what Doctor Knox has to say."

"I understand." Another uncomfortable pause ensued, and then we both began to say the same thing at the same time:

"I'm sorry … "

I am sure the effort cost him, yet he managed a wan smile. "But what are *you* sorry for?"

"Your mother's death. And what were you starting to say?"

"That I am sorry that I accused you."

"I accept your apology. But why did you think that I was the murderer?"

"Actually," he admitted, "it was not my idea."

I was fairly sure that Burke had put the notion in his head, but before I could ask, a great crash in the outer hall interrupted us.

We leapt up and charged into the ante-chamber to find Andrew wringing his hands as he stared at one of the front windows, or what was left of it. A large stone and great splinters of glass lay on the carpet under the shattered window.

I stuck my head through the ragged opening that the rock had made. Outside, there was a ragged knot of half a dozen men, one of them winding up to toss another boulder in our direction. I glared at him and snarled, "If you toss that, you and your friends are dead."

He threw it, anyway, though the men beside him tried to stop him. I roared in rage. Throwing the front door open, I went out into the street. I was possessed by a towering desire to hear all of their necks snap, and yet rather than rushing at them, I deliberately held back, lumbering toward them one lurching step at a time, my hands outstretched before me like some reanimated zombie.

Predictably, they howled in terror and scrambled off as fast as their legs could carry them. That, of course, was the result which I had intended, though my conscience still rose up, for it knew how close I had come to tearing them all apart.

When I reentered the house, locked the door and staggered back to Doctor Knox's office, definitely the worse for wear, I collapsed upon a chair and asked—begged—Andrew to bring me a tumberful of scotch, which he did before returning to the hall to sweep away the shards and splinters.

Hugh plopped down into Doctor Knox's office chair. "That," he told me, "was *awesome!*"

"If they had not run away, who knows what might have have happened?"

"I suspect that they would have provided lunch for the crows."

"Hugh," I told him with painful earnestness, "believe this of me—I *have* murdered. But not your mother—therefore who made you think so? Was it Burke?"

"Actually, no. It was Willie Hare who swore that he saw you near the house. Burke merely said—and so did MacDougal—that my mother was missing, and that I should report it to the police. Which I did ... and they had already found her body, which I was made to identify." He crumpled up into a ball of pure misery.

Granted that I am not well schooled in compassion, yet the lessons which I have learned from the Professor and Father Naman were not in vain. Clumsily no doubt, I patted the poor boy's shoulders as he sobbed.

DE MORTUIS

(Doctor Robert Knox)

It is difficult to determine whether Edinburgh's legal system is more compromised by incompetency or corruption. When I went to the morgue to examine Patsy's corpse, both of those factors functioned well on my behalf.

At one end of the chamber, several members of the constabulary argued about which district would receive credit (!) for where the murder had taken place, while on the other side of the room, standing beside the slab that held the deceased, two physicians wrangled over the cause of death. One of them, James Mellicamp, was a fellow lecturer at the university; the other was Angus McLaren, a former student of mine. When they saw me, they immediately stopped bickering.

McLaren treated me with respect; Mellicamp, likewise, but with a jealous edge, for he had often railed in public against how I supposedly "hogged" the limelight as the school's most sought-after tutor. Still, they could hardly ignore my forensic expertise, and they agreed to let me settle their debate.

McLaren said, "She was strangled." He tilted Patsy's head so I could examine the bruises along her neck. When I was done, Mellicamp stepped forward and, opening the victim's blouse, showed me the slices in her bosoms and chest that spelled out—

S i n

"That is what killed her," he proclaimed.

I studied the incisions. They were keenly etched, not ragged...all except for the deep puncture wound that dotted the "i" in the middle. I examined it more closely and realized that it had resulted from several jabs and cuts.

"So?" Mellicamp asked. "Which one of us is correct?"

"Gentlemen," I said, "allow me a few moments to study the victim. Have you a scalpel that I might borrow?"

McLaren replied, "There is one on the floor by your foot. Someone careless must have dropped it." He eyed Mellicamp with contempt.

I bent down to pick it up, and was shocked to see a monogram etched along its handle. The scalpel was one of mine. How did it get here, of all places? The thought that immediately occurred to me was that the murderer had slipped it into the victim's pocket, and it fell to the floor when they laid her down. At least, neither of my colleagues had recognized that it belonged to me, which amply demonstrated, to my relief, their lack of professional skill.

I immediately perceived that the marks of strangulation which I saw upon Patsy's throat had been produced post mortem, and that initially made me immediately speculate that they had been placed there specifically to draw suspicion toward my giant patient. But stabbing her with one of my own scalpels made me wonder whether I was not the target, instead.

I bent over the table and probed for a time, but it did not take me long to determine the real cause of death.

"Well?" Mellicamp prompted impatiently as I straightened up. "Which one of us is correct?" McLaren echoed his rival's sentiment.

I turned so that they could not see me slip the scalpel into my pocket, then, facing them (for I would not wish to miss their expressions!) I replied, "Gentlemen, you are both wrong."

THE POWER OF THE PRESS

Hugh and I had talked about Eve for a little while, but now we just sat there in silence in Doctor Knox's office. I thought that the afternoon would never end. The tedium grew so intolerable that at last, for want of anything better to say, I asked Hugh if he knew how to play chess.

Lost in thought, chin resting midway between his shoulders, at first he did not seem to me hear me. But then he raised his head and looked at me sharply. I was afraid that, under the circumstances, he might find my suggestion insensitive, but when he spoke, his tone was not unfriendly. "You know how to play chess? Who taught you?"

"Doctor Knox...but only a few hours ago. I'm afraid I am a total novice."

He grinned at me in a crafty manner. "I don't suppose that you would like to wager a bit, then?"

"I have hardly any money."

"A pity." The light in his eyes dimmed, but then he gave a good-natured shrug. "Still, it will pass the time. You're on!" He set up the board, and took a black piece in one hand, a white in the other, and mixed them so neither of us could see. "Reach in and take one."

I did so and chose black. He swiveled the board so the black pieces were next to me, and we began our chess match in earnest.

We played three games, and Hugh beat me every time. He was even better than Doctor Knox.

Heredity? I wondered.

The third time, I nearly tied him, but I missed one crucial detail, which he was swift to point out. "Still," he said, "you have got a fair instinct for chess, I think."

I thanked him as I set up the board in Doctor Knox's mate-in-one problem and challenged Hugh to solve it.

"Mate in one?" Hugh laughed. "You must be joking! Anyone could determine the answer in an instant! All right, let us just take a look ..." He glanced at the set-up, which I noted was not nearly so long as it took me to reach the same conclusion. "It can not be done."

"I think so, too. But Doctor Knox showed this to me, and assured me that it is possible."

Hugh looked down again at the board. This time, he took a good long moment to think it over, during which his eyes went in and out of focus. Suddenly, he broke into mirth both raucous and aggrieved. Choking back tears, he said, "Someone murders my mother, and here I am, laughing. What a heartless rogue I must seem!"

"No, Hugh! Sometimes I think that the only way to conquer grief is to veer off in the opposite direction."

Forcing himself to breathe deeply, he let his emotions down a notch. "That is a bit o' wisdom," he said. "Where did you learn it, I wonder?"

"That is something that you do not want to know. But what started you laughing?"

He pointed at the chess board. "I saw that there is indeed a way to solve the problem ... but it would be an utterly outrageous solution!"

"But you are *sure* that it can be done?"

"Yes. I am positive that there is only one possible way that it could be accomplished. I am also positive that most chess players, and I do mean chess *masters* would be utterly defeated by Knox's arrogant brain-twister! The man is a genius, you know! Also a bit of a monster."

I winced at that word, but Hugh did not notice.

Just then, the front door slammed. "Well," the lad remarked, "speak of the Devil, and here he is."

Doctor Knox's return, much as I had hoped it would be soon, came at a slightly frustrating moment because I never got a chance to find out Hugh's solution to the mate-in-one problem. I tried to ask, but the physician was making so much noise roaring at Andrew because of the rain blowing through the broken front window that I could never have heard the answer.

The Doctor slammed the office door wide open and strode in, cursing as he divested himself of dripping outer wear.

"Look at that!" he growled, slapping a large news-sheet on his desk (I later learned it is called a broad-side); he must have kept it inside his coat; it was mostly dry. The headline stretched across the page.

OBNOXIOUS KNOX
HARBOURS HORRORS
A TIMELY HINT
to
ANATOMICAL
PRACTITIONERS
and their
Associates—the Resurrectionists

What is our great city coming to? In pursuit of "the good of science," anatomists at Edinburgh University, led by the infamous Doctor Robert Knox, encourage Resurrectionists to commit sacrilege by violating the final resting places of our beloved mothers, fathers, sisters, brothers, uncles, nephews, nieces, & c., and stealing away their poor mortal relicts so that the anatomists may wreak gross harvests of vital organs from our departed loved ones. Let us be sure of what this means! The bodies of our kin are being stolen by Resurrectionists and sold for their paltry profit. Once Knox and his ilk get them on their dissecting tables, do they honour them with even the most perfunctory rites of passage and worship? Never for a moment! The beasts cannot wait till they rip them apart and, at best, study their innards for what they profess to be the hallowed institution of scientific knowledge.

Perhaps in some perserve fashion their reasoning can be understood, if not condoned, but anatomical research is only part of the secret. For when Aunt Brianna or Uncle Timothy are stretched out on the anatomist's slab, a decision must be made as to whether they are in good enough condition to service the demonstrations held in the university lecture hall. Many of those we love are kept in vats—yes, vats!—of preservatives until such time that some vital organ or other is required, at which time it is sliced loose and re-employed as an object of study.

Horrible, do you say? Yes, but to what end this post mortem mutilation? Does the ghoulish procedure benefit the living?

YES!

It has come to our attention that Doctor Knox is busily engaged in harvesting organs so that he may put them inside the body of that hideous monster that West Port citizens recently saw threatening that poor young man affectionately known as Daft Jamie, who has been missing ever since that night. The huge fiend has been identified as the <u>PATIENT</u> (!!!!!) of Doctor Knox, who some call BUTCHER!!!!!

Curiously, just before the night in West Port happened, a rumour began to circulate that the murderer of one Henry Clerval, whose body was found—

I stopped reading. I had come to town under complete secrecy, and yet now everybody knew that I was here. Worse, I was suspected of the murder of Henry Clerval, for which I was, of course, guilty, but now I was also a suspect in Daft Jamie's death (the town did not know yet that he was dead, but I did).

Doctor Knox answered my unspoken question. "If the thought has not yet occurred to you, then let me suggest it. You, sir, have an enemy."

Hugh interrupted. "Did you find out who killed my mother?"

"No, I did not. But I discovered how it was done."

"Yes, I am listening."

Doctor Knox was uncharacteristically tentative. "The details," he said, "are a bit gruesome. Are you sure that you want to know?"

"She is my mother—I have the right!"

The Doctor sighed. "I do not dispute that. Well, there were bruises on her neck which suggested to one of my colleagues that she had been strangled, but I studied them, and they were inflicted post mortem, which means—"

"They happened after she was already dead. I understand."

"All right ... now brace yourself. The next thing is worse. The word 'SIN' was carved into her breasts and chest. The 'S' and 'N' balanced one another just below the teats, whereas the 'i' was mid-line."

It was too much for Hugh. The poor youth threw up. Doctor Knox called Andrew, who was waiting just outside the door. It was the janitor's off-day, so the mess had to be cleaned up by Doctor Knox's hard-working assistant.

After Andrew left the room, the Doctor laid his hand on one of Hugh's. "I should have prefaced that detail, lad, by telling you that the carving was also accomplished after your mother was already deceased. She did not suffer because of it."

Hugh muttered thanks. "But if she was neither strangled nor stabbed, how did she die?"

"That is the ingenious part of the atrocity. The 'i' in the word *Sin* was actually dotted."

"Yes? So?"

"So, lad," said the Doctor, "that made me suspicious. Would a killer be that orthographically punctilious? Was he a perfectionist who could not bear to commit an etymological error, or was there another reason for dotting that 'i'?" He looked at us. Whatever one might say of the man, he certainly liked to maximize dramatic moments. "As I studied the incision," he continued, "I realized that it was actually a cluster of small, separate incisions. That is when I concluded that the dot of the 'i' was deliberately made in order to conceal the hole."

"What hole?" Hugh demanded.

"The hole made by a small-calibre bullet. Your mother was shot to death."

AN OMINOUS VISITATION

I am not sure whose eyes went wider at that revelation, mine or Hugh's. I could not determine when his mother had been shot, but it had to be late at night because it was already after dark when Father Naman and I spirited Eve away from that dreadful house.

After her daughter was taken away from her, Patsy Kensit must have decided to walk the streets of Edinburgh, for her body was found some distance away from where she had lived in West Port. Yet it puzzled me that her murderer chose such a noisy way to kill her. The shot had to be heard some distance off, yet the culprit had remained in the neighbourhood long enough to leave bruises on the victim's neck—that, of course, I knew could not have taken very long—but a great deal more time had to be involved to carve the word "Sin" into her flesh. Dotting the "i" alone, according to Doctor Knox's charactery, could not be done all that swiftly. Perhaps she was killed elsewhere and her body trundled and dumped in the Lawn-Market?

I ceratinly had questions to ask the Doctor, and if I did, I am sure that Hugh had many more, but we never got to pose them, for the front door-bell suddenly jangled.

"Andrew," Doctor Knox called, "answer that." Under his breath, he cursed whoever it was.

A few seconds later, three men entered the room. I already knew two of them. One was Father Naman. He made a subtle "shushing" gesture to me as he appeared just behind the man who had watched me in the West Port pub. Today, Deacon Brodie was soberly dressed, and when his sly eyes caught mine, he acted as if he had never seen me before.

The first of the three to enter, evidently the commanding member of the deputation, was a tall, slim, imperious aristocrat with thick white hair well-trimmed over his high forehead and crisply cut around his slightly pointed ears. A pencil-thin moustache was also white, as was a trim beardlet that bracketed his prominent chin.

Doctor Knox introduced him as Major Thomas Weir, which meant nothing to me at the time, though later Andrew told me the Major was the great-great-great-grandson of a self-proclaimed sorcerer who was also named Major Weir. He and his sister, who was his diabolical partner and his lover (!), were both burned at the stake.

I began thinking that one had but to breathe the smoky air of Edinburgh to become utterly corrupt. How my surmisal would become manifest in the present deputation I had yet to learn.

Major Weir commanded our attention. "I am here with Deacon Brodie to discover whether certain alleged medical practices at this establishment require official intervention both municipal and sacred." He indicated Father Naman. "Thanks to this Holy Father, we are here convened to learn and, as necessary, to take speedy action to halt anything illegal or sacrilegious done within these walls."

"Indeed?" said Doctor Knox. "Perhaps you have a warrant to show me?"

"If it comes to that—" Brodie began, but stopped at a harsh look from the older man.

"We have come here as a courtesy, sir. You are, after all, one of our city's leading medical authorities. If you are able to reassure us that nothing untoward is taking place within these premises, the matter will end there, and there will be no need for a warrant or any other official document or process." Major Weir's smile as he stated this would have been quite at home in the Arctic Circle.

But his smile disappeared when he turned to look at me. It was not pleasant; a light I can only describe as *unholy* danced in the dark pupils of his eyes. "You," he said, "whatever you are, go away while I speak to the Doctor."

I stood up, but not to leave the room. A wild rush of blood flooded me; I suddenly felt hot and angry.

"This is *my* patient," Doctor Knox snapped. "Since this business, I suspect, concerns him, he has every right to stay and hear what you have to say."

A milder voice intervened. "May I make a suggestion?"

"Please do, Father Naman," the Major said with a courteous nod.

"Perhaps the patient might agree to accompany me to another chamber where I would be happy to provide him with spiritual counsel."

Another nod from him. "I am chiefly concerned about certain operations that have been brought to my attention, but the patient's … spiritual salvation is also an important issue. I will regard it as a promising sign if he is willing to take counsel with the Holy Father."

Whatever Father Naman had in mind, I wanted to know, so I said I would do as he suggested.

Major Weir seemed quite satisfied, especially with himself. "While they are out, I shall question you, Knox."

The physician regarded him like a slug dirtying the path he meant to walk on. "You will address me as *Doctor* Knox, sir, or I will personally pitch your venerable carcass into the street."

"How *dare* you speak to me like that?!"

Tempers were at full strength, but I was spared the particulars of the clash. Father Naman drew me away to the front parlour and waiting room for patients. He shut the door so that we did not have to hear the clamour.

I spoke first. "You wanted them to think we had never met?"

"Just Weir," he replied. "Brodie saw us together at the pub, remember? The Major assumes that we are strangers, and for some reason the Deacon has not disenchanted him of the notion."

"I wonder why?"

"The same question has been bothering me, too. Major Weir wields a great deal of power in Edinburgh. Brodie knows better than to work at cross-purposes to him. So why is he keeping our little secret?"

"Do you think he has been paid to keep quiet?"

The priest nodded. "That is exactly what I have been thinking."

"I confess to total mystification. Doctor Knox did warn me, though."

"Warn you of what?"

"He said I have an enemy."

"Who?"

"He named no one."

Father Naman fished out a flask from his cassock, took a drink and passed it on to me. As I sipped whisky, he mused aloud. "Knox is right. I have been thinking the very same thing. Otherwise, how could the rumours have begun? I do not mean the chatter about the giant at the West Port tavern, we know how that started up."

"You mean the gossip about Henry Clerval's murderer being in town."

"Yes, but more than that." We shared another sip of scotch. "What I find especially unsettling is how Major Weir was able to trace you here."

"You told me my screams have been heard."

"True. But those who traverse a sector of town peopled by medical professionals cannot be surprised to encounter the sounds of suffering."

"The two operations I had were uncommonly late in the day."

He nodded. "That is perhaps a clue. Yet how have anonymous cries in Surgeons' Square been connected with the giant of West Port?"

We thought and thought, and then Father Naman said, "You know, Deacon Brodie has seen me several times at St. Giles. Perhaps he has been having me followed."

"Perhaps. How did you come to meet Weir?"

"The Deacon introduced me to him today. It soon became clear to me that they were going to cause you a good deal of difficulty … though it is really Knox that they're after."

"What, exactly, are they trying to do to him?"

"Shut him down," said the priest. "He is as cordially hated in some sectors of the community as he is cordially admired in other circles."

"But how can they hurt him because of me? So he is performing surgery on a great misshapen creature. How does that threaten the citizens of Edinburgh?"

"It is meant to be, or look like, a battle against the Resurrectionists."

I began to point out that in neither of the surgical ordeals that I had undergone, no vital organs other than mine own had been involved, but then a thought struck me that was so obvious I wondered that it had not occurred to me sooner.

"Burke and Hare!" I exclaimed.

He looked puzzled. "What about them?"

"They are my enemies! First they killed poor Jamie out of spite because I took his part against them. Now it is Eve's mother because we frustrated their plans to prostitute the child!"

"Perhaps. But I see two objections." He passed me the flask one more time before putting it away. "Point one—Patsy was still earning money for the MacDougal woman. Point two—even if they did murder her in some vague gesture of revenge, why would they carve her up and leave her body to be found in the Lawn-Market, rather than bring her to Knox for their usual fee?"

I admitted his points were difficult to explain away. "I need to think about it. Perhaps we will discuss this again later?"

"Perhaps ... " Father Naman hesitated. "But I have not had a chance to tell you that my sabbatical has been cut short. Tomorrow I must return to Dunkeld."

Now, more than ever, I needed his counsel, but I chastised myself for selfishness, for he had clerical duties to perform, and other souls who required his spiritual guidance. He saw my distress and pressed my hand. "When the Doctor is done with you, please come and visit me. There is a secret place in the cathedral that I will tell you about." He gave me an encouraging smile. "Meanwhile, perhaps you will be able to rely on Captain Walton. I am told that the Professor received a letter from him informing him that Walton expects to arrive in town any day now."

A tentative rap at the chamber door. Andrew poked his head in. "Would you mind returning to the office?"

We did. The visitors were gone. Doctor Knox sat behind his desk glaring at the world in general. When he saw me, he waggled a finger in my direction. "Those two are up to no good. Whatever transpires, I can ride out whatever they attempt, but your very life may be at risk."

"Why do you say that?" I was afraid he was obliquely referring to the Henry Clerval murder, but that was not what he meant.

"When they return, *and they will*, it will be with whatever legal instrument is necessary to prevent me from treating you as my patient. Without my ministrations, I am afraid that you will die. Even with said efforts, I might not be able to counter the condition to which you are prey."

"Are you giving up?" Father Naman asked.

Doctor Knox sat straight up. "*Never!* But the second operation I performed confirmed what I must call both good and bad news." He turned to me. "I thought it was going to be necessary to harvest various organs and go through the tedious, tricksy business of transplantation. But the ones you already have—liver, spleen, stomach, upper intestines—are in surprisingly good condition. Except for the ongoing bleeding that I have had to stanch, that knife-wound did no serious damage to any vital structure."

"But what is the bad news?" I asked.

"Your systemic problems are accelerating. I only perceive one possible way to reverse or slow down the degenerative process, and it would be a desperate and dangerous thing to try, for I have not yet assessed the condition of your heart. It might not be able to withstand the strain."

"Doctor," I said, "if we do nothing, how long do you think I still have?"

"Difficult to determine, but I believe we are talking about months at best, not years."

"In that case, what do I have to lose?"

"The intervening time. If we do this thing, your life could be over in a matter of days."

A long silence, then I waved it away. "You have warned me that Major Weir might stop you from treating me altogether. If we are going to try this thing, we must act swiftly."

"I must point out that it will take some time for me to rig up the kind of equipment I have in mind."

"What sort of equipment?" I asked.

Doctor Knox drew close to me. "Something on the order of what Victor Frankenstein employed to bring you to life."

"Do you mean apparatus for channeling *Lightning?*" I exclaimed.

"Exactly."

LIGHTNING

(Father Naman)

I knew that he was going to have some more bad news to assimi-
late, but this was not the time to bring it up. I kept my peace while the
Doctor answered his questions. It was Knox's opinion that restimu-
lation of his flesh and tissues by the formidable power of Heaven's
electricity would either rejuvenate or destroy him.

"I wish that I could consult the journals and notes of your late
creator," he said. "Do you think that they still exist?"

"I do not know," said the creature. "Perhaps you could institute an
enquiry to that purpose?"

Doctor Knox nodded. "I will, though we can not wait that long."

Perhaps I should have said something at this juncture, but I could
neither assess nor explain to myself how Knox's plan made me feel.
In such strange circumstances as these, there is no clear-cut map that
a priest may consult. If I offered counsel while I was thus confused,
how could I afterward reconcile it with my conscience?

At last, when the Doctor had said all that he could, and the creature
left the room to go downstairs. I followed him. There was one thing I
could do, of course, and it did not compromise any of my feelings or
misgivings, so when we got to his basement room, I suggested that
in pondering the dilemma Knox had proposed, it might be helpful for
him to discuss it with his friend, Professor MacMorris.

He instantly agreed to go and consult him, so I wrapped him in
garments that both disguised and insulated him against the prying
curiosity of strangers and the Edinburgh weather, which was growing
ever more foul.

Soon we were making our way through the storm to the dormitory
where his friends were staying.

Just as we reached the front door, someone saved us the trouble of
opening it and emerged from within into the squall.

"Captain Walton!" the creature exclaimed.

He was too bundled up, of course, for the captain to see his face, but his size was, of course, evident. The man turned to him and said, "I know that voice."

In that moment of recognition, I realized a thing that I could not have appreciated on ship-board: the difference between the way that Captain Walton looked at me and the friendly regard I always saw in Professor MacMorris's eyes, failing though they were. I knew that Walton did not bear me any of that unthinking ill will that most men harboured upon first seeing my misshapen body. He was, after all, beholden to me for saving his own life, but his gratitude stopped short of anything approaching genuine friendship. By sending me to Pitlochry, he had proved that he had my best interests at heart, yet I was well aware how much efforts on my behalf cost him, for he was, after all, the last earthly friend of Victor Frankenstein.

He wore the same dark wool top-coat he had on the last time I saw him at John O' Groats; on his head was a shiny kind of slicker-hat to ward off the rain. Clutching his collar tight to keep out the wind, which was whipping up in the usual Edinburgh fashion, he said, "The Professor told me that you are staying with Doctor Knox. I was just going there to see you."

"Well met, then. I came here to visit my friends, the Professor and Eve."

He gave me a piercing look. "You do not know, then?"

"Know *what?*" I am afraid I raised my voice.

Father Naman, patting my arm, suggested that I stay calm. "The Professor will explain," he said.

"What have you not told me?" I brushed off his hand. "Never mind, I will find out for myself."

I started to go inside the dormitory, but Captain Walton stepped in front of me, which was a risk on his part, and he knew it. But I forced myself to stop and hear him out.

"What?"

"I simply wish to remind you of your resolution, and the promise that you made to me."

With great difficulty, I controlled my temper. "Captain Walton, there is never a day that I do not think upon that. Now excuse me, I must go to my friends."

(Father Naman)

My sciatica was acting up worse than ever. By the time I hauled myself upstairs to the rooms where the Professor was staying, the creature was already there, filling the open door-way. Judging by his fierce expression, he had been told the thing that I had been keeping from him. When he saw me, he whipped round and gripped my shoulders with such force that I cried out. He immediately released me.

"I am sorry, Father," he said huskily. "I must rely upon your strength."

"What there is of it," I replied, resting heavily on my stick and wincing at the agony in my leg. "Tell me what I can do to help."

The Professor called out, "They have arrested Eve."

I knew that much, but MacMorris filled in the particulars, though the details were few enough. Deacon Brodie came with a warrant, a policeman and a witness: Willie Hare. They made the Professor and Eve submit to body searches of a thoroughly immodest nature. When he heard that, my companion growled and gnashed his teeth.

In one of the blind girl's pockets was found a locket that Hare identified as belonging to the late Patsy Kensit. Hare accused the child of stealing it from the dead woman.

"They planted it on her!" the creature howled. "Do they think she would have harmed her own mother? She was so eager to be with her!"

The Professor was distraught to the point of tears. I said what I could to console him. "They cannot fashion any kind of case against the poor girl. They must soon release her." To the raging giant I said, "Come, there is nothing that we can accomplish to-night. Let us return you to Doctor Knox."

I stumped down the corridor, trusting that the creature would follow me. I descended the stairs and went to the street door, where I paused to look, but not yet venture to go outside. Thunder rolled like great kettle-drums, and in the distance I saw jagged bolts of lighting strike an iron street-lamp again and again.

When my companion joined me, he said, "I want to visit Eve."

"And break her out of jail?"

His great hands balled into fists, but he did not answer me.

"Maybe," I suggested, "you will be able to see her to-morrow."

"Then you will go there with me?"

"I can not. I must return to Dunkeld Cathedral. But perhaps Captain Walton might be able to accompany you."

"I will go there myself," he growled.

"If you do, I am afraid that it will be at your peril."

I knew that the priest was right. I wanted to play Samson and shake down the walls of Eve's prison. But that would probably only make matters worse. I could only hope that Father Naman was correct and that they had no real case against her.

We stood inside the door for a long time gazing at the storm. Thunder split the skies, and frequent cracks of thunder and lightning sounded and flashed repeatedly. Odd, I suppose, but watching such wild weather always serves to calm me. It was a trait that I shared with my creator, for Victor Frankenstein reportedly liked to walk in the forest, the hills and the lake near his home in Geneva.

I opened the door. The priest suggested that we wait till the elements abated to some extent, but I told him,"No. I need to walk. Trust me, it will help settle me down."

"Very well … but where will you go at this hour?"

"Do not be afraid, I will not try to rescue Eve—to-night, at least. I am going to walk for a bit, and then I shall return to Doctor Knox's." I pointed in that direction; as I did, my finger aimed itself toward a corner of Surgeon's Square.

I started off at a pace that I knew the priest could not match.

Sometimes there are moments in life that flood back into one's memory with dreadful clarity. The most recent one was when Doctor Knox told me of his dangerous plan, an idea, risky though it was, that must be my only hope…but a plan that could be thwarted at any time by my meddling enemies.

The earliest moment of my life that sometimes returns to haunt me is that instant when I first opened my eyes and saw the shock and revulsion in the eyes of my father as he looked down, horrified, at what he had created.

Why does that look *still* torment me?

I call him my father because he is the closest approximation to such a being that I have. A father, *y clept*, of course, but I never had a mother.

But as I slogged through the rain-swept streets of Edinburgh, I suddenly realized that I was wrong!

When I reached the lamp-post, I clasped both hands round its shaft and prayed to my mother, the lightning, to give me one more chance at life.

Her answer came swiftly.

(Father Naman)

He charged out the door at full speed, and I knew in a flash (ironical diction!) what he meant to do.

I could not hope to keep up with him, as he well knew, so I hobbled along in his wake.

The lamp-post was only a block away from Knox's establishment, but by the time I got there, his body lay a crumpled heap upon the ground. What could I do? My options were severely limited; at first, I thought that there were two choices my meager power might be able to execute, but as I thought it over, I knew that I was wrong, for I had only one thing that I could do, and I must do it as swiftly as possible (certainly a relative concept, considering how agonizingly slowly I had to limp along, given the buffeting wind and the relentless pains in my leg).

But finally, I burst in on Knox. He was with a patient, but when he heard what I had to tell him, he moved with uncommon speed. In a matter of seconds, he and Andrew had clothed themselves against the weather, sent Andrew to the basement for a large wheel-barrow, and followed his man as he trundled it into the alley, heading in the direction that I had specified.

I pursued them, if a cripple may employ such a hasty word. When I arrived, I saw Andrew (who had neglected to don a hat) standing by the barrow with rivers streaming over his face as Knox, down on his knees, pummeled his patient's chest with clubbed fists.

Presently, he stopped striking him. The Doctor rested his right ear on the place that he had been pounding. When he rose, he saw me and said, "He is still alive!"

It was a tribute to Knox's expertise, but even more so, it was a testament to the hubristic science of the late Doctor Victor Frankenstein.

UNDER ARREST

I have seen pictures of Asian oxen so huge that it would make even me wary of crossing their path. When I finally woke—to my great surprise and relief in Andrew Napier's borrowed bed-chamber—I felt as if I had made the mistake of standing in the way of one of those gigantic Oriental beasts!

I heard someone sniffle. Andrew entered, a handkerchief dabbing at his nose. "Ah, good, you are awake," he declared, then sneezed. "Excuse me!" He handed me a folded sheet of paper. "Father Naman asked me to give this to you."

I thanked him, took it, unfolded it and read its message.

> What you did was foolhardy, but brave. Knox declares it paid off; you are healed.
>
> By the time you read this, I shall be on my way to Dunkeld. You will stay in Edinburgh, I know, at least till the Professor and Eve are reunited. After that it is my wish that you meet me at my cathedral. To avoid being seen, come at night and look for the long crack in the western wall near the River Tay. It is a leper's crawl, sometimes called a leper's squint, and it was used to enable lepers to take Holy Communion without inflicting the parishioners with their disease. Look within; there will be a message from me. Leave a reply inside the crawl, and I will find it. Enter the eldest part of the cathedral—the part that is in ruins. Here you may safely hide. Be wary of falling stones.
>
> *Your spiritual confessor,*
> Father Naman

I looked up and noticed that Andrew was still in the room. He sneezed a second time.

"You have caught a cold?"

"Yes. It serves me right for not putting on a hat when we rushed out to rescue you."

"How long was I unconscious?"

"The better part of a day." He fidgeted in his usual fashion. "The Doctor asked me to bring you to his office. You have a visitor."

I rose from bed. "I will be there directly."

He sneezed again and left the room.

I expected that I would see Captain Walton, but instead there was the oily Deacon Brodie standing rigidly next to Doctor Knox's desk, where that worthy was seated writing a medical record and patently ignoring the visitor.

When I entered, the Doctor looked up. "I am very sorry to disturb you when you should be recuperating," he said, glancing contemptuously at the Deacon, who was as drably dressed as the day that he arrived with Major Weir. Evidently he only sported bright garments in the evening. He carried a jeweled cane in one hand, which he pounded on the floor.

"If your patient requires rest," he barked, "he will get plenty where I am taking him."

I took a step toward him. "And where do you think that is?"

He backed away, turned the handle of his cane and pulled out a sword. "Keep your distance, villain! I have a warrant for your arrest."

"On what grounds?" the Doctor asked.

"First," the Deacon replied, "he may have been involved in the murder of Patsy Kensit."

Doctor Knox laughed scornfully. "Can you just imagine *him* wielding a scalpel?"

"I only said that he may have been involved. He was seen that night outside her house. There were marks of strangulation, too, which he would certainly be capable of, and of that, Doctor, you are well aware." Brodie pointed the sword-tip at me. "Before I answer any other questions, I must direct you to turn out your pockets and show me that you have no concealed weapons therein."

I saw no reason not to comply, as my pockets were empty.

"Good. Now I am going to search your room."

"It is Andrew's room!" I protested.

Andrew, who had remained with us, confirmed that fact.

"In that case," the Deacon shot back at me, "you have nothing to fear."

"True," I grumbled. "Go ahead, for all I care."

Andrew led him away.

Doctor Knox said, "I expected something of this sort to happen. Had I known it would come this soon, I still would not have counseled you to try what you did last night, but the fact that you are standing shows that you made the right decision. You must have the strength of an ox."

I had to smile at the comparison.

"Doctor," I said, "though I can not imagine that there is any reason that the Deacon can conjure up to take me away, in the event that he is somehow successful in doing so, I have something to ask you before he returns."

"Ask away."

"Something that you said yesterday stuck in my mind, concerning the harvesting of organs. I presume by that you meant that you might have had to replace one or more of mine with replacements?"

"Indeed, that was my intention," Doctor Knox averred. "However, as witness your current revitalization, it turned out to be unnecessary for me to do anything of the sort."

"But you could have done so."

"Yes. Why do you ask?"

"I am wondering whether those organs you might have been able to replace would include …" I hesitated. "…eyes?"

He studied me for a moment before replying. "That would be quite difficult for me, as I have not specialized in optics. Theoretically, though, it might be possible. Its success would depend on many factors, not the least of which would be finding a workable set of eyes. But I presume you are not asking on your own behalf?"

I shook my head.

"I have known Eve MacMorris since birth," the physician told me. "Her condition was truly the fault of her late mother."

"I have heard that that was so."

"The question, then, is which of her anatomical elements are unable to perform their natural functions. If, as I suspect, that tally includes her optic nerves, I do not think any procedure I could perform would alter her blindness."

Just then, Andrew returned, looking stricken. Deacon Brodie, whose broad features were contorted into a smug expression, entered right behind him. His two fists were clasped round something he carried in.

"Well, sir," he said, "what have you to say about *this*?" He opened his hands and placed a small silver snuff-box on Doctor Knox's desk.

"That belonged—" I caught the Doctor's warning look and shut up.

"Yes?" Brodie purred, a cat about to pounce. "Whom did it belong to?"

"It is the property," I said, "of Jamie Wilson."

"I am glad that you are honest enough to admit it. I found it hidden in a drawer in the room that you have been staying in."

"I do not believe it!" said Doctor Knox.

The Deacon turned to Andrew. "Am I lying, sir?"

Andrew blew his nose, then shook his head miserably.

"All right, Brodie," the Doctor argued, "what if you did find it down there? Perhaps the boy loaned it to him."

"No, sir. I was in the pub the night your patient tried to take it away from the lad."

I pounded my fist against the wall. "It was Burke who tried to steal it! I was making him give it back."

"That is not the way it looked to me," Brodie argued, "and Willie Hare will back me up."

The Doctor sneered. "For enough money, that sneaky wretch will say anything you tell him to. Now may I remind you that James Wilson has been missing for some time, but that does not mean he will not turn up any day now and tell you the truth."

Deacon Brodie's head bobbled. He agreed affably. "That is quite possible, of course. But I still wonder what circumstances caused his ever-so-treasured snuff-box to end up in this creature's possession."

Again I slammed the wall with my fist. "I did not take it! Someone sneaked in and put it in my—in Andrew's room!"

"Indeed? Who would want to do that? Mr. Napier? Doctor Knox? Who else lives here and has access?"

Of course that told me the only possible culprit, and the memory came back to me how, on the night Patsy Kensit died, I watched Willie Hare hand something over to Paterson, Doctor Knox's janitor. Apparently they paid him to hide the snuff-box in my bed-chamber.

It confirmed what I had suspected all along, that Burke and Hare killed poor Jamie—else how could they have possession of his snuff-box? It all confirmed my belief that the two villains were my sworn enemies.

Doctor Knox defended me yet again. "You are going to have a tough time, Brodie, proving that my patient filched this bauble. Surely the arrest warrant that you have brought with you could not be for such an infraction, since you only just found your alleged evidence. As for that unfortunate woman's murder—"

Deacon Brodie held up an interrupting hand, then produced an official-looking document, which he gave to the Doctor to read.

Doctor Knox scanned it swiftly, then faced me. "They are arresting you on suspicion of the murder of a man named Henry Clerval. Have you any idea what this business is about?"

I was too stunned to answer him in words, but I nodded yes.

"I promise that you will have excellent legal representation. We will clear you of this charge!"

Considering that we had begun our relationship with him expecting to be paid for his expertise, his offer to secure an attorney on my behalf was uncommonly generous. But though Father Naman was not with me now, I was certain how he would counsel me. I knew what I must do, and the thought calmed my soul as none other had ever done.

"Thank you, Doctor Knox," I said, "but I am going to plead guilty."

NOT ENOUGH

(?)

Here is where it ought to end, I suppose.

It satisfies all logical demands—does it not?

Of course it does.

Yet it is not enough!

There is more involved here than the mere exigencies of logic. Emotional demands also must be factored into the equation. No, that diction is incorrect. The heart's requisites cannot be classified as an "also." This core of unslaked misery cannot be relieved by jurisprudence's formal judgment and sentencing.

Blood must have blood.

And yet this lesser victory makes further revenge impossible.

Or does it...?

I knew what he liked to imbibe, so I ordered it, but again I declined to drink with him. I watched while the limited spectrum of the man's mixed perceptions and rapacious emotions played across his ever-so-readable bull-dog face.

"I thought that you would be pleased," he said doubtfully.

"I am." A long pause. "But still, it is not enough."

He did not even attempt to conceal the greedy hope that was inspired in his breast by my remark. But his face fell. "It will have to be enough, though, now won't it? He is in jail, and there he will stay till they take him out to hang him."

"Or *try* to hang him," I said. "That, I think you will agree, will not be easy."

"Not even on my own father's gallows," he admitted. "He *is* big.

But however that turns out, I do not see that there is anything more that I can do." He fixed me with a calculating stare. "But I have a notion that you have got something more in mind."

"Yes, I do."

"Then what do I do next?"

"That depends."

"On what?"

I tapped the back of his hand. "I trust you to do what you are paid for, and those you may require to help, for you must be my financial intermediary where they are concerned."

He nodded. "That is, of course, understood. But what do you mean us to do?"

"How well do you know Major Weir?"

That query produced a startling stream of invective from him. Once he was finished assuaging his vituperation, he asked me why I wanted to know.

"I have heard certain interesting rumours about his, shall we say … religious convictions?"

A crafty smile played upon his lips. "Ah, yes? And what have you heard?"

I told him. Not only did he confirm what I had heard, but he elaborated to a degree that I admit rather shocked me.

I outlined my plan, which consisted of a set of circumstances, events and contingencies. He said that it would be neither easy to put it in motion, nor certain of success, but I reassured him that he would be paid no matter what the outcome might be. That pleased him; he offered to buy me "a wee dram."

This time I accepted.

PAROLED

The jail was bleak, cold and dirty, but I had not wholly recovered from what might fancifully be called my maternal resurrection, so as soon as the cell-door lock clicked shut, I settled onto a stiff, unyielding cot, which at least bore my weight, and I soon fell fast asleep.

I do not know if minutes or hours passed before I woke, but from the little sun-light that straggled through the bars of the cell's only window, I thought that it must have been hours. The day was nearly over, and night would come presently.

A rattle, a rasp and a click; I looked up and saw a police officer with a small metal tray of food, which he set on the floor. Turning the key and locking me in again, he lost no time putting distance between us.

I was not particularly hungry, but I knew that if I spurned the unappealing mush he had brought me, I would not be served anything else, so I forced myself to eat the stuff. And after all, I thought wryly, when had I ever cultivated a palate capable of appreciating that Gallic concept known as haute cuisine?

When I was done, I lay back down on the cot. I was no longer sleepy, but it was cold, so I bundled myself up in the coarse, prickly blanket that they had provided, and began to examine my surroundings. My eyes traveled from stone to stone to stone till I grew bored. How long I would have to stay here before my trial I could not tell. I started counting the blocks that comprised my cell, but that, too, was a tedious business, and soon I gave it up.

I stood up and put my hands round the bars that shut me off from the jail's central corridor. Taking care not to make noise, I shook them to find out how sturdy they were, and knew that if I wished, with some effort I could break them apart. Not that I would do that—I had, after all, surrendered myself to mankind's justice as an act of expiation.

While I stood there, I looked past other cells and was surprised to see at the far end of the corridor an ornately-decorated folding screen that struck me as totally out of place. I noticed that a prison guard was sitting behind it. Very well, I thought, but why would he deliberately block his view of the cell? Perhaps he was also having his dinner. Some people, I have heard, do not like to be watched while they eat. Of course his meal would consist of better food than the slop that they served the prisoners. Maybe he merely wished to avoid unnecessary provocation?

It was idle speculation, of course, and of no particular significance, but I was bored, and anything that whiled away a few moments was of value. Yet it teased and jostled me, surely more than it was worth—I asked myself why, but could not come up with an answer.

I have heard that one who has been struck by lightning may experience a huge expansion of mental acuity, and sometimes, one's occult sensitivities will increase, as well. I do not know if this is true or not, but as I paced back and forth in my cell, splinters of new thoughts rushed into my mind, and odd recollected details began to occur. I did not like one of the ideas that thus visited me, and put it out of mind, for now, at least; the puzzle of the prison guard's screen also remained out of reach—but suddenly, in a baffling display of *non sequitor,* yet totally convinvingly, came an awareness of the answer to Doctor Knox's maddening checkmate-in-one problem!

A click. I turned and saw a guard opening my cell-door. "You've got a visitor," he said, and stood aside to let him enter. *What strange timing,* I thought. The idea I had disliked and set aside involved Captain Walton, and here he was.

It was the first time that I had ever seen him when he was not wearing nautical clothing. Whatever profit he must have realized on selling his ship had enabled him to purchase new garments that were quietly elegant; his light blue shirt lacked Doctor Knox's dandified ruffles, while the captain's dark blue trousers and matching long-tail jacket spoke of fine cloth and excellent tailoring, as did the new outer coat he wore.

"Good evening ... Frankenstein," he said. While we were traveling to the Orkneys I told the captain that I had decided to take my creator's name, but this was the first time he, or anyone, had ever used it, and it startled me. "I admire what you have done."

"Surely you do not," I disagreed. "You know that I am a murderer."

"Yes, but I never expected you to submit voluntarily to the rigours of justice."

"Neither did I, Captain. But now that I have, I feel more at peace than I have ever felt in my entire life."

"You know that they will show you no mercy."

"I neither expect, nor deserve none. But submission to my fate may perhaps lead to my ultimate salvation."

"Do you speak in a temporal, or in a spiritual sense?"

"Both, though I confess I am riddled with doubts about the existence of an after-life."

"Aren't we all?" Captain Walton crossed to the hard cot and sat down. "I offered to put up bail so that you would not have to wait in this unpleasant place till your trial, but they have absolutely refused me."

"I am not surprised that they would not let someone of my size and strength roam free. But it was good of you to try. Is that why you came to see me?"

He shook his head. "I am here to bring you some good news and deliver a message."

"From whom?"

"Professor MacMorris. He wanted you to know that they have set Eve free. He has taken her back to Pitlochry."

"I am so glad to hear that! In the forest, they may live a simple, and a good life." My smile disappeared. I realized that not only would I never see them again, but now they knew that their friend is a murderer.

Captain Walton seemed to know what I was thinking. "The Professor asked me to tell you that no matter what you may have done in the past, he is and always will be your friend. And furthermore, he shall tell nothing of your misdeeds to his child."

Though Professor MacMorris's generosity of spirit deeply touched me, I doubted that he could shield Eve from finding out the truth, for sooner or later, someone would broach the subject, and probably it would be Robbie Pratt. I voiced my misgivings to the captain, but he shook his head.

"Even if what you fear comes true, don't you know that you will always be her special hero?"

"You exaggerate, Captain!"

"No, I do not. When she was leaving with her father, she told me that if I should happen upon you, I should remind you that are, and always will be—these, you understand, are her exact words, which she insisted that I use—you would always be her 'sweet guardian angel'."

I did not think I was capable of shedding happy tears, but I was.

As Captain Walton rose to go, I asked him to stay one moment more.

Much as I did not want to broach the subject, I asked his pardon for bringing up an issue that had been troubling me. He asked me what it was, so I explained: "Quite some time before they came to arrest me, a rumour began to spread that Henry Clerval's killer was hiding somewhere in town."

He immediately knew what I was getting at. "Not a syllable concerning your past has ever escaped my lips," he declared. "Not here in Edinburgh, and not in the north while I was selling my vessel. Would you think me capable of that?"

"No, Captain, I would not. But let me explain why I am so concerned. Both Doctor Knox and Father Naman cautioned me to stay indoors, yet there was a time when I was seen, and that not only roused its own share of gossip, but it brought me the enmity of two villains, a man named William Burke and his partner Willie Hare."

"Who are they? What do they do?"

"I am told that Burke is a cobbler, but mainly he and his cohort Hare run a rooming-house in the West Port district. On the side, they supply bodies for dissection to Doctor Knox."

"Resurrection men, you mean."

"I do not think so."

"Then where do they get the bodies?" I let him work it out. "Oh … I see. So you think that this pair is responsible for having you arrested?"

I nodded. "They are the likeliest candidates. But how could they possibly connect me with the Henry Clerval murder? No one in the world knows about that except me and you." I saw an odd expression cross his face. "Captain?"

"I promise that I have not uttered a word of Frankenstein's story—*your* story—to anyone. But—" He paused long enough to withdraw an envelope from his pocket. He handed it to me and was about to speak when he was interrupted by the sudden appearance of one of the guards.

"You!" He said to me, unlocking the cell. "Ye're wanted up-stairs."

"By whom? Why?"

"Come along and ye'll find out."

I exchanged a puzzled look with the captain. We followed the guard, who led us up two flights of stairs to a large room filled with desks, chairs and constabulary. The officer in charge stared at me in frank disbelief and declared, "Y' must have some important friends."

"Why do you say that?"

"Because y've been paroled."

Captain Walton stepped forward. "You mean that you have decided to honour my request?"

"It's not you, it's 'im," said the officer, pointing to a man who stepped forward with an oily smile.

It was Deacon Brodie.

A CHAPELFUL OF MONSTERS

It must be evening, I thought, for instead of the sober garb that I had last seen him wearing earlier, the Deacon was decked out now in a veritable rainbow of colours, and his gaudy frock-coat was over-generously arrayed with silver buckles. This time he did not carry his sword-cane; instead he toted a musket, which he pointed at my breast. I glowered at the ridiculous little man. Musket or no, I could easily snap him in two.

"You are released into my custody. Go into that room," he said, indicating an ante-chamber where the presiding police officer had already gone.

"Lower your weapon," I growled, "and I will do what you ask."

I said good-bye to Captain Walton and entered the indicated chamber, the Deacon following behind me. The officer waiting there for me instructed me in the terms of my parole. None of it made the least bit of sense to me. Brodie was the man who had arrested me; why would he put up money for my bail?

I asked him, and he smirked at me. "As far as I am concerned, laddie, you can stay here and rot. I am just the messenger boy."

"For whom?"

"For Major Weir. We will go to his home. There I will gladly turn you over to him."

I understood part of the puzzle now. The Major possessed both money and power; his influence and wealth enabled my bail to be set—yet he hardly knew me, and the one time we met, he displayed no friendly feelings toward me. What was his motive for freeing me, then?

Stinging rain pelted us as we ventured into the street; cold air from the Pentlands clashed with a keening wind that was blowing in from the sea beyond Leith. Brodie aimed his weapon in the direction we were to go and stayed behind me as we walked north and west along George IV Bridge. Far above us, Edinburgh Castle loomed down on us with a baleful yellow glare.

After several blocks, he told me to halt. Coming up next to me, he pointed to a tall grey stone pile set off from the street by steps with iron railings that descended to a wide flag-stone patio. "The Major's house," he said, going to the door and knocking. The portal swung open and we entered.

Inside, a liveried servant bowed to Deacon Brodie and attempted to acknowledge me politely, but the sharp involuntary intake of his breath suggested that the task taxed his social reserves. He ushered us into a drawing room where perhaps two score of elegantly-clad ladies and gentlemen were seated in cushioned chairs that all faced the front of the room, where there was a raised platform in the manner of a small theatrical stage. On it was one chair and a large mirror in a polished wooden frame, its reflective surface tilted away from the company.

Major Weir wore a long velvet open coat over a black formal suit. His long white hair flowed freely over his wide patrician brow, and his grey moustache had been waxed; its edges pointed like needles. He approached us, a frown of disapproval turning down the corners of his mouth. "Brodie, you are quite late. The Reverend has long been waiting to begin." He gestured for the Deacon to take a seat; he did so, not before shooting an angry look at the Major. Weir then led me off to one side, out of sight of his guests.

The old man thrust a large glass of whisky into my hands. "It has been aged for thirty years," he said, "so kindly do not guzzle it. Sip it slowly and savour its excellence."

I thanked him, but I doubt that he heard me. He was already mounting the platform.

"Esteemed friends," he said, "it is my privilege and honour to introduce to you the legendary Reverend Thomas Aquinas Porteous!" In the midst of a round of applause, Major Weir sat down and a tall, saturnine gentleman with the air of a conjurer took his place. He wore a turban and great robe with zodiac signs and cabalistic symbols worked upon it in gold and silver thread.

Andrew had mentioned Porteous to me, and gave me a copy of one of Edinburgh's news journals, where I read about the man. Porteous styled himself a holy man and seer, and though members of the clergy attacked him in print, his vaunted ability to foresee both past and future made him much sought after for both public and private audiences.

Addressing the assembly, he immediately admitted that he had his detractors. "To them I proclaim that I am only doing God's good work. I do not exact a fee for my labours. Voluntary contributions are welcome, but never required."

He sounded sincere enough, but I could not help but regard him as a practiced, clever fraud. Still, the man was impressive. His gestures were graceful and smooth, his voice deep and pleasant; it lulled one's senses, though mine already were in that state, for after all, I had sampled enough of Major Weir's scotch to know that it was far superior to the raw stuff Burke and Hare were used to.

I sipped it as Porteous invited a young lady onto the platform. He held her hands, but did not look into her eyes, as I would have expected him to do. Instead he tilted the mirror and told her to gaze into it; as she did, he watched her reflection, not the woman herself. He then began to tell her remarkable things, each of which she verified, often with a surprised gasp: moments from her childhood, her secret passions and dislikes, details of her private life that one could not imagine anyone knowing except for herself. Lastly, he foresaw details of her future.

She went back to her seat to much acclamation, and one by one, each spectator was granted her or his time with the seer. The performances were similar to the extent that everyone who came forward was taken by the hand and told to look into the mirror, but after that we were all made voyeurs and eaves-droppers to new secrets sometimes trivial, but often daring.

But when it came to predicting the future, I noted that the details Porteous claimed to foresee were always vague, but on the whole pleasant.

Major Weir appeared at my side. "It is your turn now."

"No!" I said. "No one needs to hear that my future will end on the gallows."

"I have arranged this entire evening for your benefit, and the law has placed you into my custody. You will do as you are told." He snapped his fingers in my face and walked off, which was just as well for I nearly answered him by snapping his neck. My fists opened and closed convulsively. But I was still, after all, under arrest, so I walked unwillingly onto the platform and met the Reverend Thomas Aquinas Porteous.

Shocked gasps, exclamations and imprecations when I appeared; a woman screamed. I bit my lip to stop the growl that was starting up in my throat. Deacon Brodie saw the danger before Weir did, and he hurried to my side and handed me another large glass of scotch, which he urged me to drink. I swallowed it in one gulp and demanded more. This time the Major satisfied my demand, then he and Brodie stepped off the platform and left me with the Reverend Porteous, who approached me and said, "Do not be afraid, my son."

"Do not try to clasp my hand," I warned him.

"Very well," he said accommodatingly. "Here is a chair. Please be seated." Close up, he looked a lot older than he seemed at a distance. His eyes were a blood-shot green, and there was a fine network of veins across his hooked nose and square chin that suggested that he was no stranger to alcohol. He smiled at me with less cordiality than he had affected for his earlier subjects, but the difference was minimal; he was too professional to display the dislike for me that I knew he felt, and of course it was mutual.

Because I am so much taller than the other people he had on the platform, he needed to swivel the mirror to such an angle that the rest of the spectators were necessarily cut off from seeing what I was able to observe, and that was a veritable panorama of the room behind me. At the back stood Major Weir, with Deacon Brodie seated nearby. Off in a shadowy corner I caught a glimpse of someone else standing and watching me, but it was too dark to see who it was.

"I perceive a little boy," Porteous said to me suddenly.

"Where?"

"I mean, there was a little boy somewhere in your past."

"I do not know any little boys," I protested.

"Poor lad! You meant him no harm, but he did not know that. I see that he is struggling with you."

"*Stop!*" I commanded.

"If you fear the shadows of your past," Porteous replied, "do not look into the mirror. Look into my eyes." I did. His pupils were cat-like, and he did not blink. He seemed to be staring directly into my brain. "Now," he continued, "the boy is gone. I see, instead, a young woman. She is beautiful, but very sad."

"I do not know who you mean."

He squinted as if to make his visions clearer in his mind. "You only saw her on two occasions. Her name was … yes, it is coming … Justine."

I decided to say nothing.

"Who is this now?" he asked. "Another woman—Elizabeth Lavenza—no, I am wrong. That was before she married and became—"

I stood up and hissed at him between gritted teeth, "Speak that name at your peril!" Behind me, murmurs and whispers told me that the crowd was suddenly uneasy.

Porteous took a step away from me. "I only see shadows of what has gone before. But since they are visions of unhappy times, I will not subject you to any more of them." He tilted the mirror so I could no longer see into it. "You may leave the platform, sir."

A voice I recognized as Deacon Brodie's shouted, "But you have not told him his future!"

"It's murky and unclear," the reverend said, abruptly quitting the platform.

Major Weir led his guests into a large chamber where tables were set with a plentiful array of fish and fowl, fruit and vegetables, sweetmeats and alcohol, all to be consumed standing. I thought that the evening's "entertainment" was done, and would have preferred to go off somewhere and be alone, rather than have to endure the many stares and whispers directed towards me, but the poorness of prison fare had left me hungry, so I heaped food on a large plate and went to a corner where I could stand as far away as possible from the others as I ate.

For a time I was left to myself. No one disturbed or provoked me. But then a raven-haired lady in a green satin gown crossed the room and stood much too close to me. Her dress was cut immodestly low at the bosom, and I saw that her eyes were the same colour as her garment.

"You are a dangerous man," she said. Her husky voice clearly approved of the sentiment that she had uttered.

"I am not a man," I replied.

"You are proportioned like one, and generously." She stared at me with naked candour.

Just then, one of the servants struck a small bell and Major Weir announced, "It is time to go to the chapel." The guests put down their plates, and I supposed they would all adjourn and go to St. Giles or perhaps Greyfriars Kirk, but none of them donned cloaks or hats; instead, carrying their liquor glasses with them, they merely quit the room.

The woman in green gently tugged my arm. "This way ... the chapel is in the cellar."

I was about to pull away from her, but the Major joined us and, taking my other arm, said, "Excellent! I see that you have met Justine. She is my favourite disciple."

I winced on learning that her name was one that I associated with guilt.

"Follow us," the Major told me. "Our service can not begin without you."

"Allow me to stay in this room. I am not schooled in man's religions, and might cause you embarrassment."

"You are better prepared than you think," Justine reassured me with a distinctly unsettling smile.

Major Weir nodded. "She is telling you the truth. Now come along."

They led me down a long, winding stair almost as narrow as the one that leads to Doctor Knox's attic. We came to a corridor whose floor was composed of flat grey stones. Several doors opened off this hall; one standing open revealed a large store-room filled with wine bottles; another was closed and secured with an iron pad-lock. Along one wall there were three barred cells, though no prisoners were within. I hoped that the Major was not thinking of putting me in one of them.

A wide door off the stone-flagged corridor led to the chapel, a long stone oblong with an arched ceiling. The guests, who now wore black robes with cowls that covered their faces, were seated on long wooden benches. The place was very dark. Several black candles positioned between altar and pulpit provided flickering light that made shadows dance off walls whose plaster surfaces were covered with frescoes hideously unlike what one might expect to see in a church—studies in gross venality, filthy animal acts, and scenes of cruelty and blood-shed.

The Major smiled icily. "You see? You fit right in here, sinner, do you not?"

He told me to follow him forward. Justine kept her grip on my arm. Soon, we reached the long dais that bore the altar and pulpit; centered between them was a small platform that rose perhaps half a foot from the flooring. Directly above it, suspended from the ceiling were long chains that ended in a pair of metal bracelets.

"Turn around. Face the worshippers," the Major said, pulling on his own black robe, which, unlike the others, was ornamented at the breast by a large crimson cross. "That is correct—now stand on that platform and raise your arms."

I saw what they meant to do to me, and I shouted, "NO!"

Major Weir's eyes blazed. Sanctity, or what sometimes passes for that commodity, self-righteousness, was practically a physical force in this man. I had been bound over, legally and perhaps morally as well, to this strange, intense autocrat.

"Do as I tell you—*murderer!*" he snarled.

A rotund man suddenly stepped onto the dais. Throwing back his hood, he revealed himself to be Deacon Brodie. His firearm was aimed at me.

"If you do not listen to him, you are dead," Brodie murmured. Then he raised his voice and bellowed, "Is this prisoner resisting the terms of his arrest?"

"Go away!" Weir barked at him. "I can handle him without your oafish assistance."

Brodie muttered a few choice words, but got off the dais.

The Major addressed me. "Frankenstein, you have a choice." Again I was startled to hear my chosen name aloud. "Cooperate, and you will be treated with more consideration than you deserve till your trial and its inevitable aftermath. But if you refuse, that buffoon Brodie will immediately return you to prison."

"If he does not shoot you along the way," Justine whispered.

My heart pounded, my thoughts raced. Neither Weir nor Justine could imagine how close they were to disaster.

In the woods near Pitlochry, my intention had been to honour the promise that I gave to Captain Walton never again to commit an act of violence. But Edinburgh's dark events were undermining my resolve.

With Father Naman's counsel, I have striven to repress my rage, but he is gone now, and so are the Professor and Eve. Still, I told myself, Weir has taken you away from prison, fed you well and provided you with superb scotch. What if he does truss you up and turn you into a dumb show for the edification of his congregants? Is that so terrible? Are you not inured to degradation?

Murderer though I be, yet I was still an innocent, for as I had no idea of what the Major actually intended, I stepped onto the small platform and raised my arms. Justine swiftly shackled my wrists.

Major Weir began the service, leading the worshippers in the stranger prayer I have ever heard. My knowledge includes a smattering of Latin, and this sounded like that tongue, but none of it made any sense; for all that I could tell, they might have been reciting it in reverse.

Deacon Brodie's loud bray dominated all of the other voices. He stood close by the dais.

When the prayer was over, the Major embarked upon a sermon, the theme of which was sin and expiation. The corners of his mouth turned down, and his lips curled and puckered as if tasting something disagreeable, and every time he spoke the word "sin," he glared at me in righteous wrath. I recollected that the word had been etched into Patsy Kensit's corpse, and could well imagine this madman performing such an horrific deed and feeling justified in doing so.

While Major Weir roared and ranted, Justine placed her warm hand upon my chest and began to describe tiny circles against my flesh with her finger-nails. With the flat of her other hand, she began downward strokes that did not pause when her hand reached my waist. Nor did she stop there, but touched me intimately through the material of my trousers. I had never before known such a sensation, it was both exhilating and upsetting, for it awoke the phantom of passion, a phenomenon that I lacked the ability to experience other than vestigially.

Meanwhile, the Major's sermon took fire from the nightmare visions which he invoked, and the congregation reflected his perverse ecstasy in groans, shouts, screams and grunts better suited to a barnyard than a chapel. Abomination was their true creed, and I noticed that the Major's rhetoric contained no negative references to Hell. I supposed that would be blasphemy to these folk.

Justine kept doing things to me that were so vulgar I shall not detail them. But at length she frowned, for she could not bring about the impossible. I told her as much, but, brushing a strand of dark hair from her eyes, she smiled at me and said, "There are many ways to bring about what Boccaccio calls 'the Resurrection of the Flesh.' I know them all."

As Weir's sermon reached its climax, Justine grasped my shirt and ripped it in half, baring my back. Major Weir, who had just stopped preaching, stepped over to his "favourite disciple" and, producing a blunt rod from the folds of his robe, handed it to her.

I saw, at one end of the rod, short, thick, knotted strands of leather. I recognized it from my time aboard Captain Walton's vessel; it was what British sea-men call a cat with nine tails.

The sensation was a minor rudeness at first, nothing like the pain I had known in Doctor Knox's surgery. With a sharp intake of breath, I thought of my manifold sins and braced myself to endure the beating. But the whip depends upon cumulative damage, and the ninth crack of the lash stung and made me bleed.

I told Justine to stop. She paused just long enough to find out whether her efforts had wrought any change in me. Discovering that they had not, she set upon me once again.

By now, the vile chapel had turned into a place too repellent to describe. I will not call their behaviour beastly, for that would slander innocent animals, even the savage ones. One all too familiar word came to mind—Weir's congregants were monsters, though unlike me, they wore their hideousness within.

Justine wielded her scourge with deadly skill. The bitter immediacy of pain brought a new thought along with it: this punishment was no random act of chance, it was part of a plan devised by the determined enemy that Doctor Knox had warned me about. Could that be him at the back of the chapel, watching my humiliation?

My endurance had finally come to an end. I shrieked, "Enough!" and yanked down my chains, along with a great chunk of ceiling. Plaster dust choked me; I coughed, then thrust Justine to one side and wheeled on Major Weir. "Unlock me," I told him, smacking the floor with the chains dangling from my fore-arms.

Women began to scream.

"Never, fiend!" the Major roared, and, snatching the whip away from Justine, began to hit me with it wherever he could.

I lifted him off his feet and hurled him like a potato sack against the pulpit. His head struck it hard and he slumped to the floor with a groan.

Shouts and screams of "Murder!" Twisting around, I saw the crowd rushing to get out of there. Pushing and shoving one another, climbing over anyone unfortunate enough to lose their footing, knocking anyone aside who were blocking their escape, the "congregants" effected their escape.

Justine watched me in fascination and fear. "Go," I told her. "I will not hurt you."

"Thank you." She quickly left the chapel.

Suddenly, I heard a sharp snapping sound behind me. I turned and saw Major Weir's dead body in the arms of a kneeling Deacon Brodie.

"You murdered him!" he said.

"I did not! *You* just broke his neck. That is a sound that I know all too well."

The Deacon rose and aimed his musket. "And who is going to take your word over mine?"

But he did not know how fast I can move. He fired one shot that lodged in my thigh.

It was the last thing that Deacon Brodie ever did.

Not that I cared, but I do not think that he suffered much. My rage, now that it had been loosed, was of such an intensity that he surely must have swiftly gone into shock.

I dropped what was left of him on the altar.

RESCUE FLIGHT

I felt absolutely no guilt at killing the Deacon. Had his aim been better, he would have done the same to me. Yet I knew that I had broken my word to Captain Walton, and could not bear to think of ever standing face to face with him again.

I heard shouts from above and feared that the servants or guests had summoned the police. I found the keys to my shackles in Major Weir's pocket, used them, snatched the musket from Deacon Brodie's dead fist and ran up to the front entry-way. There was, indeed, a constable just inside the door. When he saw my size and the weapon I carried, he stood aside and let me pass, but once I hurried into the street, he began to blow a whistle.

My leg throbbed, my heart pounded, my brain was enflamed. Cold rain pelted my naked back, stinging it where the lash had stripped it of skin; what remained of my shirt after Justine ripped it apart was mere tatters.

I was close to the northern shore of the castle lake, so I headed there long enough to pitch the musket into its murky waters. The thing had already been fired, and I had no bullets, so it was of no use to me.

Where should I go? I wanted to return to the medical school, but surely that was the first place that my pursuers would look for me, and I did not want to place Doctor Knox, or for that matter, Andrew, in any sort of legal jeopardy, which my unlooked-for appearance might bring about. Suddenly I knew just where I must go—and instantly regretted that I had thrown away the gun.

Twice before I had gone to Tennent's Close, but each time I had been coming at it from the south. Though my notion of Edinburgh geography is fuzzy, I thought I must be somewhere north and east of the West Port district, so I headed south and west. Soon, the streets narrowed. That, plus the darkness and the weather's fury worked in my favour, for I was able to pass from one patch of shadow to another and seldom needed to hurry past the feeble glow of a street-lamp. I saw almost no one along the way, and those few that I did see had their heads down and covered, and did not notice me.

I made a few errors, but presently began to recognize where I was, and directed my steps with greater conviction. Perhaps half an hour elapsed by the time that I found the street and house where Hugh had lived with his mother.

I pounded on the door. The dour, dark-haired MacDougal flung it open, and began to curse, but when she saw me, her mouth gaped and her imprecations ceased. Gathering her wits, she took a step backward and said, "They was bettin' y'd coom." She beckoned for me to follow her down a dark hall and into a candle-lit room furnished meagerly with an unpainted wooden table, and a few chairs; its dark corners were thick with dust and cluttered with heaps of rags.

Burke sat across the table from Hare. They were drinking beer and playing cards. I yanked Hare to his feet and growled, "You have been telling lies about me!"

"Hold, off, now, I had a reason!" he exclaimed. "Brodie paid me to, and if'n I refused, Burke here would've. Money's money, lad, but there was no malice meant...was there, Burke?"

"None in t' world. Willie's got a gin'rous heart. But look at y', man! Y'r soakit sark is split apart! Coom, sit thee doon. MacDougal, fetch blanket! Willie, pour a wee dram for t' puir gent!"

I glared at the unsavoury pair. I still thought that they must have murdered Jamie Wilson and Eve's mother, but much as I wanted to knock their heads together, vengeance would not bring back either of their victims, and there were questions I needed answered, so as they might just prove useful in that regard, I collapsed onto a chair and thanked MacDougal for the scratchy blanket that she draped across my shoulders and back. Hare handed me a mug of bitters, which, though I had already drunk too much that evening, I was too agitated to refuse.

"So what did they put y' through?" Burke asked. "Willie and me've heard wicked things about the goings-on at Major Weir's."

"You have heard true," I said, thinking that what I witnessed there might even shock this wicked duo. "But how did you know that I was going there?"

Hare sat down and refilled his mug. "We were part o' what the Deacon called a contingency plan."

"Meaning what?"

"Meaning he thought y'd either escape before he c'd bring y' t' Weir's house, or summat arterward. Deacon said if'n y' did, y' mought show up 'ere."

It did not make sense. "Brodie's a mercenary like the two of you. He told me he was only Major Weir's messenger-boy, and as soon as he delivered me there, he was done with me. Why would he pay you to take part in this so-called contingency plan?"

Burke shrugged. "Willie an' I were wond'rin t' same t'ing. Best guess is somebody else was paying off Brodie."

"Who?"

"No idea, lad."

I did not trust them, but in this instance I was inclined to believe them. I meant to find out just what Brodie wanted them to do as part of his "contingency plan." I drained my mug, let my head droop, and passed into a supposed slumber.

They waited for a long time to see if I would rouse, but I did not budge. Hare prodded me, gently at first, then sharply. I muttered an incoherent protest, slumped so my head and arms sprawled across the table, and began to snore.

Burke sent MacDouglal from the room, then tested my condition to his own satisfaction. Achieving no result, he stopped jostling me. "Drunker'n sin," he judged.

"Aye," Hare agreed. "Why n't y' burk'im proper, and 'ave done with it?"

"Are y' daft, man? Or are y' fixin' t' sell me carcass t' Knox?"

"I wouldn-a t'ink o' sich a t'ing!"

"Burk'im!" Burke declared scornfully. What if he woke while m' hands were round his neck? 'Twould take more'n yer skinny arse t' keep 'im doon, and then we would both be goners."

"True, Bill, true. We had best proceed wi' t'original plan."

"Aye, let's do't."

They left the room. I waited for a few seconds, then got up and followed them. I saw them at the far end of an unlit corridor leading further back into the house. While I waited to make sure that they did not see me, I glanced round in the other direction and noticed that MacDougal was at the front door peering into the rainy night. I assumed that she knew what they were up to, and was acting as their "look-out."

The two men were no longer in the hall. I hurried after them and entered a chamber dimly lit by a taper and strewn with straw. On an improvised pallet, Eve's brother Hugh lay pinioned by Burke and Hare. The latter sat on his legs while Burke hovered over him blocking his nose and mouth.

"Get off him!" I shouted, grabbing both of their throats. Burke immediately put his hands over his head. I released him and he backed away. Hare did the same, but when I let him go, he spun round with a dagger in his hand.

"If you throw that," I told him, "you had best be accurate. I have already killed Brodie."

The conspirators exchanged glances, and uttered colourful curses. Burke grumbled, "If that is the sitch'wation, our labours then are for naught. Dead men pay no debts. Willie, put away t' blade."

Hare did so. I examined Hugh to see if Burke had hurt him, and as I did, they ran from the room. The boy was awake, but disoriented. I smelled liquor on his breath.

"What's doing?" he asked thickly.

"What's doing," I replied, "is that Burke and Hare just tried to kill you. Come away, it isn't safe for you here."

While he gathered his wits and his few possessions, I returned to the front room to demand that they tell me who had hired them to kill Hugh and make it look like my fault, not that I thought they knew who was behind Brodie, but they were gone and so was MacDougal.

I ran back to the youth's room. "Hurry!" I urged him. "Those villains will soon return with the authorities."

Hugh shook his head. "Bill and Willie go t' police? Not bloody likely—they'll go t' pub an' roust up mob."

Even as he said it, I heard the buzz of angry voices rapidly approaching. I ran to the front door and saw that we could not make it out of the close, so I went back to Hugh's room, picked up a chair and smashed a window that we swiftly passed through and retreated into the night.

The rain had let up and now was no more than a fine mist. We skulked through wretched alley-ways and streets feebly lit with lantern-light.

Hugh noticed me limping. He paused to look at my leg and saw the blood from Brodie's bullet. He tore off a strip from my already tattered shirt and bound it tight round my thigh.

"Something I learned from Professor MacMorris," he said. 'Twill have t' do y' for now."

Though the mob soon stopped following us, several times we had to duck into dark door-ways to avoid being seen by citizens and night patrols. By now, I had to assume that I was being hunted for Weir's and Brodie's deaths. I asked Hugh where we should go, and he said, "We've got t' get y' out o' Edinburgh."

PART THREE
At Dunkeld Cathedral

TRAVELLING NORTHWARD

We worked our way north and west as swiftly as we could; when Hugh saw how fast I can move, he let me carry him on my shoulders for a while. (Yes, I still ached more thann a bit, but anything that would help us leave town faster was worth the discomfort.) By the time that the morning's chill promised the imminent appearance of the sun, we had skirted the Firth coast-line some miles west of Corstorphine. I set Hugh down beside the river.

"The water narrows here," Hugh said. "Let us try to find a boat and row across." He led me now, for he knew this part of the country much better than I did. We found a row-boat tied to a small pier, untied it, tangled a few small bills onto the rope for the boatman's trouble, and rowed it across to a place just north of a village, so he said, called Dunmore.

His attitude towards me had changed radically since our first meeting. While the process started, as I have told earlier, on the same day that we met, it was considerably helped along by the fact that I had just saved his life. There was, after all, no need for him to accompany me, a fugitive from the law, in my flight from Edinburgh. As we moored the row-boat and the rim of dawn began to peep over the ridge of the Pentlands, I asked him, "Now that you have also left town, where do you mean to go?"

Hugh shrugged. "Haven't thought that far ahead. But I am thoroughly sick of the city."

(Hugh Kensit)

You can not live in Edinburgh and not have morality crammed down your throat and up your arse. There was a time when I lived with my sister and the Professor, and one thing that I will say in his favour is that he taught us—*demanded*, actually—to think for ourselves, and though, over the years, I have done a few things that I am not proud of, I never committed any serious crimes, and that is because at a very early age I drew the conclusion that you could sometimes bend the rules a bit, but breaking them was just a cheap, cowardly short-cut. Life is a game with tough rules, but I do like challenges.

My poor mother now, when it came to immorality, lived what they call a paradox. She was one of MacDougal's girls, yet every Sunday me and Eve went with her to prayers, which she preferred simple and to the point. The only time I ever saw her being feisty was when a visiting clergyman brought a choir with him to sing hymns, and that was way too Catholic for my mother. When the service was done, she strode up to the preacher, tapped his chest (and not lightly!) and said, "How dare ye fill m' lugs (ears) wi' Pope-songs?!"

Anyway, the point of this rumination is that I am not saying that I am proud of some of the things I had to do to keep a roof over our heads. It was Deacon Brodie who tipped me that cheap rooms were being let by Burke, and I knew that meant they would not be in Fountainbridge. But what I did not know, though I soon found out, was that everything that Brodie, Burke and Hare were involved in was as tainted as rotten mutton. Still, when they put me in the way to earn a few shillings from time to time, I took them up on it, but the things I had to do for them were minor infractions compared to some of the things that I suspected they were up to.

Which brings me to this strange creature called Frankenstein—it seems that he is a murderer, yet though I have seen him angry, and a fearful sight that is, there is at other times a touching gentleness about him, and what is more—the word seems strange—an *innocence* that has stirred me to help him escape.

It was almost day. Hugh said, "Soon there is going to be a lot of commerce in and out of town, which means that there is a good chance you could be seen and reported, and if that happens, they will be sending out troops after you. You had better wait till dark before setting out again."

I admitted the wisdom of his plan. I saw a barn a little distance off and thought it might be a good place to hide. "But what about you?"

"I will only slow you down. And on the road, travelling in your company might prove risky…no offense intended."

"None taken." He accompanied me as I headed toward the barn. "And where will you go, then? Have you decided?"

"Pitlochry, I suppose. It is the only place that comes to mind. If nothing else, I can say hello to my sister."

"How will you get there?"

"There ought to be a coach that I can catch at some town near here."

I stopped and laid a hand on his shoulder. "Hugh, you could do worse than live with the Professor. He needs a strong set of arms to chop fire-wood and do other chores. I know that you two regard each other with negative feelings—"

"Not as much as all that," he broke in. "I know that he is a good man."

"Then if you make an effort—?"

He laughed. "Why not? I have no other place where I might go."

We entered the barn. I found a rampart of hay to lay down behind.

"Where will you be off to when it gets dark?" he asked.

"Dunkeld. Do you know where that is?"

Hugh thought for a moment. "It is in the same general direction as Pitlochry, but further east, I think. Also it is a little closer, maybe forty-some miles from where we are now. A lot of hours to walk, though."

"Not so many for me. I can cover such a distance in a single night, if I know which way I am headed. Which I do not precisely know."

"Dunkeld is the next village over from Birnam, so if you head in the direction of the River Tay and the infamous Birnam Woods, you will get to Dunkeld eventually. So why do you want to go there?"

"I need to speak with Father Naman…if he will, after he hears what I have done."

(Hugh Kensit)

When we ran away from town, I do not suppose he knew I lack the cold, hard cash to pay for a ride to Pitlochry. The small payment I left behind for the row-boat depleted my budget, but I felt it was right to pay for the inconvenience the boat owner would endure getting across the Firth to reclaim his vessel (which I left within view from the other bank). So the first thing I meant to do after I left Frankenstein was to "borrow" a horse from whatever farm had one available. I will try to return the animal after I am done with it, or at least I will let her find her own way home, for horses know how to do that.

I wished him well as we said good-bye, and started to go, but then I turned back and asked him when he had last eaten.

"Yesterday evening," he said, "at Major Weir's."

"'Tain't good t' travel on an empty stomach." I reached into my knap-sack and took out a loaf of bread, which I broke in half and handed to him, then I rummaged and found a chunk of cheese, which I sliced a piece off with a dirk that I had stolen a few weeks back from Willie Hare. (He was convinced that Burke filched it.)

"Thank you, Hugh. I will eat them later, before I start on the road."

I said good-bye a second time, but then curiosity got the better of me and I stopped long enough to ask him whether he had ever figured out Doctor Knox's checkmate-in-one problem.

"I think so," he said, as he rested against a hay-stack. "It seems wrong, but … I can only think of one way to solve the problem." He told me his solution, which was the same one I had come up with. I nodded. "I am impressed. That was one difficult poser that Doc Knox set for you. You have got yourself a good mind there, lad."

He laughed sardonically. "I suppose it is a gift from my mother."

I stopped in Perth long enough to water horse and rider, and then it was a straight push north. As the afternoon blended into evening, I switched to a trot, then steadied her to a walk as we reached Pitlochry's main street. Dismounting, I saw Professor MacMorris emerging from a store with a bag of groceries. I was surprised to see him alone, and wondered where Eve was.

I set the food aside that Hugh had given me, for I was not hungry. I was in considerable discomfort from the wounds that had been inflicted by Brodie's musket as well as Justine's scourge. My body craved rest, but my mind was trapped in a labyrinth of shame, suspi-

cion and guilt. Father Naman had told me that my craving for abso-
lution could only be attained if I made my peace with the will of
God—

I use the capital letter "G," yet I am deeply skeptical of the
embodied deity embraced by the priest's faith. Still, his sincerity
kindled a passion in my heart; I so *want* to believe that I may be
forgiven for my latest deeds of violence. When I killed Deacon
Brodie, I have said that I felt no remorse whatever. But now, like
Claudius, Shakespeare's murderous Danish king, I was suffering a
barrage of second thoughts. Never mind that the Deacon was a hypo-
critical scoundrel who had broken Major Weir's neck and told Burke
and Hare to kill Hugh and see that I was blamed for it; never mind,
either, that he had shot me. It was not my place to be his judge, jury
and executioner; I could have easily disarmed him. Once, aboard
ship, I had told Captain Walton of the agony that I felt when I slaugh-
tered Frankenstein's innocent bride, and it was no lie … so, with
equal honesty I must admit to myself that I had thoroughly enjoyed
destroying Deacon Brodie.

How could I confess *that* to Father Naman?

And if this was not sufficient cause to rob me of my sleep, I was
tormented as well by the rumours that had led them to arrest me
for Henry Clerval's murder, Jamie's snuff-box planted in my room,
the secrets imparted to the Reverend Porteous—the great malevolent
web crafted by an anonymous enemy. I only knew one man capable
of wreaking such revenge, but he lay dead and buried in the Arctic.

Somehow I managed some fitful hours of slumber. I would wake,
peer out and see how far the sun had traveled along its celestial arc,
and when I saw that it was still day-time, I forced myself to shut my
eyes again, though that was easier than shutting off the flash and
flood of ideas half-formed, half-denied. But at last it was dusk and I
sat up.

The first thing that I did was to eat the bread and cheese that Hugh
had left for me. The crusts were hard, the core of the loaf a little stale,
but it filled me enough to get to my feet and, with some reluctance, I
left the barn's comforting warmth. The storm and its aftermath were
finally done with, but a fine sleet still slashed at me, and the air was
unseasonably chilly. When Hugh and I left Burke and Hare's house
precipitately, the broken window we squeezed through was too tight
for me to hold onto the rough blanket MacDougal had given me. As

I began my journey to Dunkeld, I spied some home-spun hanging nearby, went to it and helped myself to a blanket that I pulled round my shoulders as a make-shift replacement for my ruined shirt, which I peeled off and meant to throw aside.

But as I did, I noticed that my one remaining breast pocket had something stuffed inside it. With some difficulty, I withdrew it and saw that it was a small sheaf of paper, which I unfolded and began to examine. It was Captain Walton's letter from his sister. While visiting me in my cell, he had handed it to me to read, but before I could do so, the guard had appeared and summoned me to Deacon Brodie's custody.

I read it and saw why the Captain had given it to me, and what he intended me to read.

With a heavy heart, I refolded it and put it back in my pocket.

INTROSPECTION

Dunkeld was closer than Pitlochry. Originally, I had estimated a journey of six or seven hours to get there, but I had not reckoned on the weather, or my imperfect knowledge of how to find its great cathedral. When I was Doctor Knox's guest, I had examined a map that Andrew loaned me, and studied the village's approximate position, but our partial circuit of the coast-line north of Edinburgh had taken me too far west for me to be sure how far to the north and east I must aim in order to put myself true.

I went both north and east, as I thought that I ought. (Verbal echoes like that delight me!) I began my journey with my customary brisk gait. Avoiding the road, but staying as close to it as I could, I kept working up and to the right, until my efforts at length were gratified when I came upon a road-sign that showed me that I was indeed heading in the correct direction,

High winds and needle-points of rain found me out. relentlessly smacking my face. I would reach Dunkeld later than I had thought. But it was September, and the long days were beginning to dwindle. The sun would come up again much too soon, and I had to find the town, and, more important, its cathedral, where Father Naman had assured me that I could hide myself from the eyes of strangers.

I do not know my birth-day. That word, of course, is only tangentially applicable to me. But in whatever manner one elects to consider the date on which I was brought into existence, I do not know precisely when it was. On the long voyage from the Arctic Circle to the Orkneys, I had occasion to question Captain Walton on this topic, and he did remember that Victor Frankenstein had said that the culmination of his toils took place (these were his exact words) "on a dreary night in November."

The length of the preceding sentence reminds me that in trying to tell this, my latter history, I have managed to acquired *en passant*, as they say in chess, a modest facility with words. But though language, I think, is one of the greatest gifts ever devised, as with all benefits, it comes with a price. I have discovered that the act of setting down one's thoughts is an activity that demands order and coherency. Communication requires syntactic logic; that is surely evident, but it is so easy to become all snarled up in the very words that we attempt to employ to render us lucid.

Put simply, words are addictive. It is like going into a forest and becoming so enraptured with the trees and flowers and long grass that we turn aside from the trail, and become hopelessly lost.

What I am trying to say is that because I do not know my day of "birth," I can not precisely calculate how old I am, and that has long disturbed me. Why am I not sure, perhaps it is somehow involved with my quest for knowledge and its far more elusive sister, wisdom.

On my long hike to Dunkeld, after I had travelled for some hours, I decided that I must take a few moments, at least, to rest, for I was beginning to feel weary in a way I had not before experienced. It was as if some great pressure were being brought to bear against my chest.

I came upon a shack in the forest, which I approached cautiously, but since I saw neither light nor chimney-smoke emerging from it, I risked entering and found it empty, mercifully dry, and comparatively warm. There was a small, hard cot, a rough-hewn chair and low table, and a horse-hair blanket, the latter being a mixed joy for me, for it felt both comforting and a trifle irritating. Still, I pulled it round my shoulders and was glad for it. I found a candle, tinder and a scraping tool that enabled me, after several frustrating attempts, to strike a spark and light the wick.

I did not mean to stay long, but sitting in one place for a time allowed my many aches and twinges gradually to dwindle, and as I rested, the heaviness in my chest began to abate.

As I sat, a succession of thoughts and impressions played upon me, most of them the same considerations that had been running through my mind for the past few hours. Were I to classify them, they would fall into two categories.

The first and more peopled, so to speak, concerned those persons who had become vital influences upon me. Consider the importance of their impact, if you will, upon a creature who had so long been scorned by the human race that little was left in its heart but rage, sorrow, and a thirst for revenge. Collectively, they have helped me to change my nature, if such a thing is possible—though, considering the events in Major Weir's chapel, I am all too aware that my nature may be unreclaimably corrupt. Yet those beastly devil-worshippers sorely provoked me … if any excuse can be countenanced for giving in to that rage which caused so much misery to Victor Frankenstein.

As I sat warming myself in this shack in the woods, I thought about my benefactors, and my enemy, as well, and wondered how it could be possible for human nature to run such a gamut. Captain Walton, though truly not a friend, showed me a compassion that I have seldom known, and because of him, I resolved not to die by mine own hand, but to live in hopes of rendering some good service to the race that I have so instinctively distrusted.

Professor MacMorris, and his daughter, of course, became my first true friends, and their faith in my goodness still astonishes me, purchased, as it were, with such small favours that I performed for them anonymously. That they could not see me was both a relief and a sorrow, for I feared that they would spurn me if could they see how foully misshapen I am. Intellectually, I know that they are too good to succumb to such base instincts, but my deep-rooted, dearly purchased pessimism works against me. Thinking about Eve, I wondered whether Doctor Knox's quest to find and study my creator's note-books would yield results. But if she ever regains her vision, I do not think that I possess the courage ever to let her set eyes upon mine ugliness. In a small way, Eve's brother, Hugh, has also had a positive influence on me, as have dear Andrew Napier, and in his own self-involved fashion, even Doctor Knox has shown certain mercies.

But surely the most profound impact upon my mind and spirit have been effected by Father Naman. Though I still can not claim to embrace his religion, and am still quite skeptical about the concepts of deity and spirit, I am perhaps a little less so when it comes to the latter term, and that is partly thanks to the Professor's gently insightful nature, and partly to the astonishing healing skills that the priest possesses.

In his faith, he countenances miracles, some of which I have read about in his sacred testament. Who am I to say whether there is not something miraculous in the way his guidance and counsel have helped me in my quest to subdue my own violent nature? That I have not altogether succeeded is apparent in those events at the chapel which I have recounted, and yet, in mine defense, I do believe some credit is due for the forebearance that I practiced ever so much longer than I could have done in the earlier incarnation of that creature fashioned by Victor Frankenstein.

As I rose up, blew out the candle, and prepared to venture back into the blustery night, I knew with poignant intensity that I could not hope to assuage my conscience or tormented spirit until I stood before Father Naman and told him of my new transgressions. If he could absolve me of my sins, then and only then could I ask him to tell me the truth about my determined enemy.

REDEMPTION

And then, suddenly, far off across the rolling meadow, there it was, its enormous bulk standing out stark against the glow of early dawn—Dunkeld Cathedral.

But as I drew nearer to its stony oblong exterior, I saw that there was something very wrong with it. Fissures in a few high sections of the building's walls let through patches of pale sky pinpricked with cold, twinkling stars. I walked in a rough circle round the edifice and everywhere I saw crumbling buttresses and eaves borne down by centuries of disuse.

Close by a lawn that sloped down to the banks of the River Tay I came upon a narrow vertical crack in the eastern face of the cathedral. This was the leper's crawl, or squint, that Father Naman had told me about. He said that if I came to Dunkeld and looked within the fissure, I would find inside it a message from him waiting for me. I groped about inside the crawl and found a cylinder of paper with writing on it, which I unrolled and read.

> Friend and Penitent, do not be amazed. The cathedral dates back to the year 1260, and much of it is in great disrepair and is unsafe to walk through. Sections of it, however, have been reclaimed for worship, and in the eastern gable there are sturdy cells where you may safely wait, for it is unlikely that any of the locals would go there. You will know this section because of the irregular reddish streaking on the surfaces of the walls, relics of the Culdee monastery that predated the cathedral's construction. I have learned that there are riders from the south seeking you, therefore stay within. I will find you.
>
> Yr. Spiritual Counsellor,
> Father Naman

That sensation of pressure in my chest had come back, making it hard for me to get air into my lungs; I began to sweat and felt nauseous. Best conserve my strength, I thought. I entered the cathedral and groped my way within in the dark, heading, as best as I could tell, in an easterly direction. I had not thought how hard it would be to see, or I would have taken along the candle that I had used in the shack, or perhaps one of the lanterns which I had noticed earlier in the barn, though if I had done so, I do not know how I could now have lit it.

At length my hands encountered a door-knob; I turned it and found an opening, which I went through and, still feeling cautiously about me, perceived that I was in a small, empty chamber. I sank down with my back against one of its rough stone walls. It was warmer here than it was outside, and I was worn out both emotionally and physically. The ruin, I suppose, must have its share of rats and insects, but vermin tend to shun me, and so I soon fell into a troubled sleep.

Andrew strapped me down upon the operating table whilst Doctor Knox stood close by me with his scalpel poised. I knew that this was going to be my last operation. On my left, Father Naman stood, his hand lightly resting over mine to comfort me.

Knox began to cut into my flesh. I howled. My wrists strained against the thick leather straps and the steel clamps that held me to the table. The pain, though less severe than before, was bad enough. No, I was wrong, it was only just beginning. Sudden agony arced up like a bolt of electricity; I felt it tingling against the priest's warm, dry skin where his fingers were touching me.

He spoke to me. "Think upon the sufferings of Our Lord! What are these necessary trials compared with the thirty-nine lashes and the cruel spikes that pinned Him to the Cross?"

I tried to bend my thoughts to the priest's counsel, but his words did not hold the same conviction for me that they had for him. Besides, the taut lines of the surgeon's face commanded more of my attention. He seemed to be trying to tell me something, but I could not make out his words. Knox's lips moved, mouthing one phrase again and again, but I could not hear it because Father Naman's litany drowned it out...and suddenly I was in the waterfall again, but when I was sure that I was going down for the last time, someone pulled me up to the surface, and flames leapt up hot and high. All around me, great blocks of ice looked down. I approached my funeral pyre, but a low moan not far off stopped me. I knew it was Captain Walton, but how and why would he be here with me at the North Pole?

He was near death, but I nursed him, and he rested through the long Arctic twilight. I found the letter he had written to his sister and look! He wakes! His lips repeat the same words that Doctor Knox tried to tell me, but this time I hear them clearly: "No audience ... no audience ... "

But now it is no longer the Captain's voice, it is Victor Frankenstein's. Again he warns me—

"VILLAIN! THOUGH MY BONES LAY IN ARCTiC ICE, YET SHALL I RETURN AND BE REVENGED ON YOU...DEPEND UPON IT!"

A distant murmur of voices woke me up. A faint ray of sun showed me that I had chosen my sanctum well; by the reddish striations I noted along the walls of the cell, I realized that I had managed to find one of the chambers that Father Naman described to me in his note. The place was perhaps eight or nine hundred years old, yet its roof was still intact.

The services, barely audible where I hid, lasted for a short while, then I heard footsteps and voices, and after a time, all was silent. The worshippers must have departed.

I rose, left my cell, and headed toward the part of the cathedral where I thought the services must have been held. Soon I found a chamber filled with various historical artifacts: a monolith that, according to a plaque positioned next to it, was as old as the great slabs of Stonehenge. Along the room's other wall, I saw a sarcophagus carved in the likeness of a fierce warrior, one Alexander Stewart, the Earl of Bachon, which the inscription stated was known as "the wolf of Dudenoch." I should not have liked to engage him in combat; he looked nearly as big as me, and he was represented as wearing a full set of armour. In one wall I saw a long vertical aperture that I realized must be the interior opening of the leper's crawl.

Close by to this room, I found a chapel. On the wall just right of its entry-way hung a sign identifying the cathedral's priest and the title of his next sermon, *Through a Glass Darkly.*

The chapel was empty. I went back to the cell that I had slept in, but as I encountered no one there, or for that matter, in any other place in the cathedral, with some misgivings I stepped outside and saw that it was late in the afternoon; I had slept through the morning and most of the rest of the day.

In the fading light of a dying sun, I saw Father Naman making his slow, halting way in my direction. His sciatica must be particularly bad today, I thought, for he leaned heavily on his walking stick as he limped along painfully. When he saw me standing in the door-way, he called out, "You should not be outside!" As he spoke, his stick skittered over a rough edge of one of the flag-stones that made up the path, and he fell forward. I tried to catch him, but the effort brought back the pressure to my chest, and I winced. The priest sprawled flat on his face. With difficulty, I walked over to him, picked up his stick, examined it, then knelt by his side.

"Father, are you hurt?"

"Not severely, but I can not get up again by myself."

I helped him to his feet, propped the stick under his arm, then, clasping him by the hand, asked him whether he would listen to the catalogue of my most recent sins.

"I am pleased that you wish me to," he said. "Of course I shall— but grant me the favour of accompanying me within, where we may employ one of the church's confessional booths."

I said I would and followed him inside. It was quiet in the chapel. No sounds drifted in from the outside world. He motioned me to a booth against the left wall. I took my place within, and he sat down next to me. A thin screened partition divided our compartments.

"Now," he said, "confess to me your sins."

I told him what I had witnessed and endured in Major Weir's perverted version of a chapel. Though my back still smarted with the punishment wrought by Justine's whip, the immediacy of that night of horror was no longer with me. In my mind's eye, I saw it like some distorted reflection in the Reverend Porteous's mirror.

When I was done recounting the events that closed Major Weir's infernal service, the priest shook his head wearily. "I think that if the world had but left you alone, none of your many sins ever would have been committed."

"That is probably true, but I have tried to let go of my rage against past injustices. I have spent much too long of my life and energy doing that, Father, and all that it won for me was further pain, grief, and self-loathing. But coming to these recent events, I ask myself whether I might not have endured the torment that Major Weir's worshippers inflicted upon me."

He shook his head. "They treated you like an animal. The meekest among us would have risen up, my son...may I call you that?"

"It is somehow appropriate."

"Then listen to me—you did not murder Major Weir, and as for Deacon Brodie, it was clearly self-defence."

"But had I controlled my anger, he might yet have lived. I could have taken away his weapon without destroying him."

"Or he may have killed you for trying." He uttered a doleful sigh. "How often my brethren and I have wrangled over points of conscience and forebearance such as you raise. To be flesh is to be weak. Even if you bear some responsibility for what afterward occurred—and I do not think you do—but even granting that you might, true penitence will surely expunge these deeds from your spirit's reckoning."

"Father," I said, looking at him sadly, "I truly hope that what you say is true."

And now that I had unburdened my conscience, how to begin? Equilibrium was a comforting thought. Would it not be easier to bury the past? To pursue my thirst for answers would change everything. Perhaps I should pretend I knew less than I really did. For I was weary; the effort of *doing* seemed an unnecessary burden. Yet it was against my nature, my *old* nature, perhaps, but I only knew part of the truth, and I needed to know it all.

I quitted the confessional. He joined me as we strode along the cathedral's draughty corridors. "Father," I began, "you may remember that I told you how Doctor Knox warned me that I have an enemy?"

He pressed my hand. "Indeed, I do. But do not forget that you also have friends."

"Yes, but it is of my enemy now that we must speak. Let us go outside and talk."

"That is not wise. We should stay inside, so no one will see you."

"I have been inside all day," I replied. "The cathedral is ill-lit, and I have had quite enough of darkness. Besides, I am finding it difficult to breathe, and I need fresh air. The town is a little way off, and services are done, so I do not think anyone will happen by. I will risk the fresh open air for a few moments. Come, sit on the church steps with me."

Reluctantly, he followed me outside. We sat down with our backs resting against the front door's outer archway. Off in the distance, I heard hoof-beats. "Since you mean to speak of your foe," he said, "permit me to ask about your feelings concerning him. Are you angry? Do you seek revenge?"

"Appropriate questions, Father. The spiritual journey I have undertaken has been hard; despite remorse for my past, it has not been easy to tame my savage instincts. But though I lost my temper at Major Weir's, in the case of my enemy, I no longer crave vengeance. All that I feel for him is pity."

"That bespeaks a generous spirit." As he spoke, he regarded me with an oddly focused curiosity. "So have you found out who he is?"

"I know his name."

"Tell it to me."

But before I could reply, the hoof-beats, which had grown progressively louder, now clattered upon the paving-stones of the path leading to the cathedral. We looked up and saw Hugh vaulting from his saddle. Tethering his steed to a thick bush, he swiftly approached. The lad was dressed the same as he was the last time that I saw him. He must have been on horseback all, or most of the intervening time.

He pointed accusingly at Father Naman. "This man is not the priest of Dunkeld."

I nodded. "I know that, Hugh. A sign in the chapel tells the title of today's sermon. The man who preached it is someone called Father Bredder."

"Joseph," the priest replied, "is an old friend of mine." "He did speak today instead of me. You may recall that I have been on sabbatical. During that time, Joseph has functioned in my stead."

Hugh poked him. "Look, whoever you are, I asked people in Pitlochry, and everyone says Father Bredder has always been Dunkeld's spiritual leader."

"I did not say he was not. I have been his guest while in the vicinity, and I took on some of his duties. Joseph and I went to seminary together."

"I do not doubt that," I said. "You call yourself Father Naman. I suspect you chose that name because it is an English variant of *niemann*, the German word for nobody."

He smiled. "You have grown clever. You are correct, I adopted Naman during my travels. My true name in the Church is Father Dolorosa."

"How sadly appropriate."

"Indeed, my son. But before this young man interrupted us, you were about to tell me the name of your enemy."

What is it about Edinburgh that nurtures men of double deed? I remembered the old story of Deacon Brodie, the father of the man that I slew. Brodie, Major Weir, and even Doctor Knox—a surgeon all but worshipped by his students, a physician capable of easing pain and restoring health who yet turned a blind eye toward bodies purchased for his dissecting theatre that were either snatched illicitly from their graves or, worse, murdered by Burke and Hare for profit.

At least the priest was not a native Scot.

"My enemy, Father—which, of course, you know—is *you*."

He looked as if I had slapped him. "How can you say that? Have I not counselled you, always and ever to the good? Have I not taken your confession twice, and each time advised you wholly for your betterment?"

"Indeed you have. Which is why I was so slow to interpret odd things that I saw and heard."

Hugh interrupted us. "All right, whoever you are, what have you done with my sister?"

"Eve?" I exclaimed. "What do you mean by that?"

"When I reached Pitlochry," Hugh said, "I happened on Professor MacDonald. He told me that Father Naman had journeyed up there and told him and Eve how you had been arrested, but somehow managed to escape from Major Weir's custody. He believed that you would come to seek refuge at Dunkeld."

"This is so," the priest stated. "The girl wanted to be here for you in case you should come. She argued with her father till he gave in and let her accompany me in a coach to Dunkeld."

"Where is she now?" Hugh asked.

"She is sleeping inside the church."

"I will go get her." The young man started inside, but I stopped him.

"Not yet, Hugh," I said. "There are things which I need to talk about with this man, and I think that it would be better if Eve did not hear them."

"Does that include me, as well?"

"No, I want you to stay." I gestured for him to sit down with us, and he did.

"So," the priest asked, "do you intend to tell me what you saw and heard that you claim led you to regard me as your foe?"

"I will, but I also have questions to ask. The one now uppermost in my mind concerns the things that Hugh says you told the Professor and Eve—how are they possible?"

"What?"

"I know that you anticipated my arrival here at the cathedral, Father, but that was no certain thing, inasmuch as I was a prisoner. I was released into Major Weir's custody and taken to his house to participate in wickedness. Now how could you have learned of my escape from Major Weir? Supposedly, you left Edinburgh for Dunkeld before I was even arrested. There simply was not enough time for you to discover what had happened to me and travel up to Pitlochry with the news."

"Bad news travels fast," he said.

"So my escape was bad news?"

"That is not what I meant. How else could I have known what happened to you?"

My smile was grim. "You never left Edinburgh—that is how. You were at Major Weir's 'party' and saw that charlatan Porteous tell me about my past. Later on, you were in the cellar chapel when I broke free of my chains."

"You *recognized* me?" With that question, he confirmed what had been till then only a suspicion, one that I had fervently hoped he would somehow put to rest.

"No, Father, I did not see you. I only noticed someone lurking in the shadows at the rear of the theatre and the chapel, but could not tell who it was. Only now did I hazard a guess that it was you, but your reaction tells me that I was right. When the charlatan displayed knowledge of my sins—I was and am convinced that he had been let in on my secrets. Who could have informed him? And what about the rumours concerning Henry Clerval's murderer that had begun to circulate round town? Clearly, someone who knew my past wanted me punished. Only you and Captain Walton are privy to those details, but he would never have revealed them to a soul."

The cleric slashed the air with one hand, though it was not curled into a fist. "Do you realize what you are accusing me of?! The secrets of the Confessional are sacrosanct! I would sooner die than reveal what you have told me."

"I neither doubt nor dispute that. But long before my first confession—on the very first day that you approached me in Pitlochry forest, you were well aware of the evil deeds that I had once committed."

"How could you possibly tell whether I did or did not possess such knowledge?"

"With hind-sight," I answered him. "Before I knew how, I realized you bore me malice. Just before one of my last operations, Doctor Knox said that as there was 'no audience,' he would give me something for the pain. That revealed to me the reason for the screen in his operating room. You were standing behind it, watching me suffer."

"No! I was monitoring your penance! Do you not recall the compassion I showed you?"

"Yes, I do. That confused me. For a time, I refused to accept that you could possibly be my enemy."

"What changed your mind?"

I withdrew the letter from my pocket that Captain Walton had allowed me to read and handed it to Father Dolorosa y clept Naman. He opened it and began to read.

"So who is this man?" Hugh growled. "Do you know?"

I nodded. "I have had but one enemy all my life, and his name is Frankenstein."

"Frankenstein? But I thought that was you."

"I am a thing without a name. I borrowed my creator's."

"No," the priest objected, looking up from the letter. "Your creator is the Lord God. He and He alone has the power over Life and Death."

I said sourly, "Some men think themselves entitled to such mastery. The man who made me was one. Now he lies buried in the Arctic."

"If he is dead," Hugh wondered, "then how can he be your enemy?"

"By proxy, as it were. My maker told his dark history to Captain Walton, and he retold it in letters that he sent to his sister in England. She, in turn, made copies and sent them to Victor Frankenstein's younger brother." I waved my hand, indicating the priest. There was no mistaking him now. Despite the beard that masked the jaw, he had the same lips, the same brooding eyes. "Before this man became either Father Dolorosa or Naman, the man was—and still is—Ernest Frankenstein."

He made no effort to deny it. Instead, his mind, as it were, drew inward, and though he spoke aloud, to hear his words was virtually an unintended act of intrusion. "My brother's memoirs dismissed me as 'gentle, ill, of no severe application.' "

Gentle? "Perhaps," I murmured, "he would now change his mind."

"Perhaps." He handed me back the letter.

Hugh shook his head. "I do not understand how he could have gotten Knox to do his bidding. Say what you will of Doctor K., he's no one's tool."

"Oh, but he can be, if you pay him well enough," Ernest Frankenstein said. "But it was not just money. When I told him about my brother's creature, he became truly interested in the case ... he relished the challenge. So Knox and I made a pact. I said that I would do my best to placate Major Weir and Deacon Brodie for as long as possible. In return, he afforded me a portion of the revenge that I sought."

"Did that include murdering Jamie Wilson?" I asked.

"I did not kill that poor boy! It was Burke or Hare, or both of them, though I cannot prove it."

"But what about the snuff-box? Did you arrange to have it planted in my room?"

"You should know that I would never have stooped to such mendacity! My intent was to find some way for you to be punished for your past crimes. That ungodly pair must have found some way to have the snuff-box smuggled into your bed-room. I do not know how."

"I do. They paid the janitor Paterson to do it."

"But what about my mother?" asked Hugh. "Do you know which one of them killed her?"

"It could have been either," the priest said. "MacDougal had but to say the word that Peggy was not earning her keep, and off they would trundle her to Knox's surgery."

"Father," I declared mournfully, "both of us know that that is not what happened."

A lengthy silence. Three pairs of eyes darted from one to the other, and then the young man glared at me.

"So this is what you did not want my sister to hear."

Clutching his walking stick, the priest rose shakily to his feet. I saw Hugh going for his knife, but I put my hand over his and stopped him from drawing it. We were all on our feet now. I felt the returning pressure in my chest.

"Hugh, give him a chance to explain."

"Explain?! This proper bastard murdered my mother!"

"Not in cold blood!" the other protested. "She was coming at me with a knife!"

"What? My mother?!"

I had to stop the young man from doing bodily harm to him. "Let him tell us what he says happened that night."

Hugh glared at him. "Very well. I'm listening."

The priest stood up and, putting a few feet of distance between himself and Hugh, leaned upon his stick and addressed me. "You recall the reason why the two of us had to go to Burke's house that evening?"

"Yes. Eve wanted to spend some time there with her mother, but the Professor did not want her staying in such an unsavoury place. I promised I would go there and fetch Eve, if she would allow it. But you knew that I suspected Burke or Hare, or both, of murdering Jamie, so you persuaded me to wait across Tennent's Close while you tried to persuade the girl to come back with us. Several minutes elapsed, and then you emerged carrying her because Eve was asleep."

He shook his head. "She was not asleep, she had been drugged."

To my surprise, Hugh accepted it without question. "So that is what they were up to! I should have known better!"

"What are you saying?" I asked. "If you had any idea of what they were planning for your sister—"

"Good Good, no!" he exclaimed. "It was all intuitive, and I usually disregard hunches and the like … but I kept feeling that Burke and MacDougal were up to something, I just could not figure out what it was."

"For my part," said the priest, "I had no idea how vile that MacDougal woman is. She meant to add your sister to her stable of loose—" He abruptly stopped himself.

Hugh understood his sudden reticence. "I am well aware what my mother did for a living. But she never would have permitted MacDougal to ensnare her own child."

"In her right mind, lad, she would not, but when I encountered Patsy that night, she was a veritable mad-woman!"

"I can't believe that!"

The priest approached me. "I learned many things about that house-hold from Deacon Brodie. MacDougal made sure that all of her 'girls' became addicted to opium or other equally lethal substances. She controlled them with a system of rewards and punishments. That night, Patsy Kensit was capable of whatever desperate action McDougal demanded, and when I tried to take Eve away, she would have stabbed me had I not defended myself. That is the truth, young man."

Hugh nodded to show that he had reluctantly accepted the priest's word. "Very well. Where did you get the gun?"

"There was one in the room where Eve—"

"Never mind that for now," I interrupted. "I want to know what happened afterward. We took Eve back to the dormitory, but her mother by then was already dead?"

The priest nodded.

"But Doctor Knox told me and Hugh that her body was found some distance off, and it bore both post mortem bruises and incisions. Explain all that!"

Standing was more than he could manage. With difficulty, he sat down and rested against the stone arch of the cathedral's entry-way. "It was all thoroughly unpleasant. I consulted Brodie, and that rascal devised a way to make it look like she had been murdered by a religious maniac. I did not see the earlier stages of the scheme, though I would guess the supposed marks of strangulation were made by Burke's hands, but when he and Hare brought her in their cart to the designated place, I was waiting there, unseen. Or I thought no one saw me, but it turns out there was a fraudulent 'blind' woman who witnessed what I did afterward. I warned Brodie about her later, but I suppose she decided to remain silent, for I heard nothing more of her. At any rate, after Burke and Hare took Patsy's corpse ouf of their cart and went away, I proceeded to do the gruesome knife-work on her myself, for before I became a priest, there was a time when I tried to follow in my brother's path and in my studies, learned how to wield a scalpel."

"Do you carry one around with you?" Hugh asked him with some uneasiness.

"No. Brodie paid Paterson to sneak out one of Knox's surgery."

There was a lengthy silence. I had more to ask, but in the scant remaining sun-light, though it was difficult to make out the expression on the priest's bearded face, I got the impression that there was something more that he needed to say. I was right; when he resumed speaking, it was in a low tone, more to himself than for my benefit, or Hugh's.

"She was already dead. The blood-work I did on her does not prick my conscience, but I am reminded of an earlier time when I did kill, and still regret it. It was only a bird. I was a medical student at Ingolstadt—"

"Your brother studied there," I said.

"Yes, with Krempe, Professor of Natural Philosophy. I had a room with a balcony where pigeons roosted. Their unmusical cooing disturbed both my studies and my slumbers. One morning, I peered out of the window and saw that they had built a nest with a pair of eggs in it. I thought I must discourage them for remaining on that ledge, so I pushed open the sash, frightened away the birds and, grasping a poker from the fire-place, jabbed it into one of the eggs. I had expected the point to be stained yellow when it emerged, but to my horror, it was bloody. I closed the window and wiped off the poker. Later, when the parent birds returned, they made an awful noise. I rapped the window-pane impatiently, but instead of flying away as they always did, they began, instead, to hurl themselves against the glass again and again and again. Had it broken, they surely would have attacked me.

"From this I learned that even the most timid creatures, if roused, are capable of ferocity. I vowed that I would never again commit any such act of violence, and soon after I realized that I was better suited to the church than the halls of science. But when Captain Walton's sister sent me the record of my brother's tragic folly, something inside me snapped."

"And so you determined to come to Scotland, find me, and exact revenge for my many sins against your family."

"Yes."

"But though you had ample opportunity to cause me harm, yet you held back. Ostensibly, at least, you became my trusted spiritual counsellor. Why?"

More than any other question I had posed, this was the one that most I needed to hear the answer. It was deeply tormenting that he had dealt with me as a man of double deed: a role I could not countenance him performing with good conscience, and whatever one might think of his acts of duplicity, he was at heart, a man of the church with deeply moral convictions. I could but conclude that this was one more spiritual burden I must somehow expiate: that my sins against his brother had led him astray from the path of righteousness.

A look of sorrow and regret came upon his countenance as he began to reply, but he had only time to utter a few words when he was suddenly interrupted by a new voice.

"Willie, where are y' now? No, don't tell me—I can find y'."

It was Eve. She came out of the cathedral, clad in a simple white peasant's blouse and a yellow skirt that swirled about her in the evening breeze. With that instinctive sharpness of hearing that I had come to know she possesses, she tread carefully across the entry-way to my side. That she could discern the sound of my breath was not remarkable, for I still laboured against that heavy pressure in my chest which had slowly returned whilst I spoke with the priest.

She hugged me energetically, and that told me that no matter what she may have heard of my misdeeds, her feelings towards for me had not changed. (Doctor Knox, have you pursued my query?) Seldom in my life have I felt pure joy, but I did so then.

"Eve!"

"Hugh? Be that you, laddie?"

"It is. Are you all right?"

"And why would I not be? Do you not find me amongst friends?"

"One friend, anyway," her brother murmured, glaring at the priest.

A strange look appeared in Ernest Frankenstein's eyes. Gone was that sadness that I had seen there a moment earlier. His gazed intently at me and then Eve and for the first time I saw the face behind the mask. This man was indeed my enemy.

Yet I was determined not to reveal the naked truth to Eve, not if I could avoid doing so. I asked her whether she knew that someone in Edinburgh had been working against me, and she said she had heard both her father and Captain Walton surmise as much.

"Father Naman," I said, "has discovered the truth, and was just about to tell it to me."

"Ah, then, I shan't interrupt." And with that, she sat down beside me.

"Father," I said, "you were about to tell me about my enemy's true nature."

"Was I now?" When the priest stood up, so did Hugh, but I kept my place beside Eve. A tense interval elapsed, then, with a shrug, he smiled. "Why not, then? Very well. The man was caught in a virtually unsolvable dilemma. On the one hand, he wanted to hurt you. On the other, he saw in you both an unexpected innocence and a suffering spirit that yearned to do penance. Thus he was utterly conflicted. What should he do? Avenge his brother? Uphold his family's honour? Or extend the solace of Christianity … even though you are not of the faith."

A sudden sharp inspiration from Eve. She got to her feet, and so did I. "Willie," she said in some temper, "what do y' take me for? A total witling? This priest is talkin' about himself, is he not?"

"Indeed, I am! This sweet guardian angel, so you call him, is a monster and a murderer."

"You confessed me!" I protested, "What is more, you absolved me of my transgressions."

"All but one."

"Yes. Justine Moritz. Why does she mean more to you than your own father and brothers?"

His answer was torn both from his throat and his heart. "*Because I loved her!* Father and Victor did not take me seriously about it, but I have never loved any other woman, and she had feelings for me, as well. We—" He paused, stared intently at me, then resumed. "Yes, I want you to know this—she was going to have my child! Thus you are guilty of yet another death."

I went cold. Knowing that both Eve and Hugh had heard it was nearly as dreadful as learning about this new horror that I had unknowingly committed.

"How I deserve your hatred," I murmured.

"I knew that she was innocent," he continued. "I swore that I would find out who let her take the blame for little William's death, no matter how long it might take me."

"Well, you succeeded."

A morose smile. "So you knew Justine meant something more to me. More intuition?"

"Oh, no. Once Doctor Knox told me and Hugh about the autopsy he'd performed—"

"On whom?" Eve suddenly interrupted.

Hugh snapped at her. "Don't interrupt!"

She nodded. I was relieved that she let it go without argument. "Father," I said, "once I knew about the—" I groped for a euphemism. "—the *modus operandi* (though I knew Eve understood that tongue), I remembered a strange thing that you did when I told you about … the woman and the—item of jewelry—details that I now know you had already read about."

"True," he nodded, "but I wanted to—needed to—hear it from your lips."

"So do you recall what you did then?"

His brows knitted as he tried to recall the incident. "Ah, now it comes back to me," he said. "All of the things that you told me— which I may not, of course, repeat—most of what I heard did not make me change my mind about the ordeal that you had meant to undergo in Knox's surgery."

"An ordeal," I noted, "whose rigours were predetermined by yourself."

Eve, whose language sometimes could be rather blunt, surpassed anything I had heard previously from her lips. "It was you, then, who told Knox not to use anaesthetic?"

"Some priest, eh?" Hugh muttered.

With a bleak smile, he answered them. "Yes, it was indeed my intent to make him suffer. However, I had come to know him by then, and though I tried to shout them down, I was already having second thoughts. But when you confirmed what I had read about my beloved, all mercy was banished from my heart and spirit. I declared to you that whatever agonies you would suffer under Knox's scalpel might serve as fair and proper expiation for your sins. Note that the significant word here is *might*."

"Understood, Father," I said, "but you are omitting one cogent detail."

"Which is what?"

"When I told you about Justine, you rose to your feet in a rage." To spare Eve from possible alarm, I silently indicated the priest's walking stick. "You pointed—something—at me."

A grim laugh. "I did not point it. I aimed."

Hugh was aghast. "Do you mean that thing—"

With a nod towards Eve, I put my finger to his lips. "Just before you got here today," I told Hugh, "Father Naman tripped. I restored—*that*—to him, but not before making sure that it was, uh … empty."

"What *are* you two talking about?" Eve snapped. We tried to ignore her, but to no avail.

"I'll tell you what they are trying to keep from you, lass," the priest said. "My walking stick is really a fire-arm daubed all over and thus disguised with peat-moss and mud."

"It's a gun?" she cried, stepping backward swiftly, something she normally was too cautious to do without knowing the terrain.

"Be calm," I told her. "It is not loaded."

"It was not when I tripped," the cleric admitted. "But I saw you examining it before you handed it back to me. While we sat in the confessional booth, I reloaded it."

That was too much for Hugh. "And you call yourself *a man of God*!?"

"Yes, boy, I do. You have heard everything that he and I have said. I am indeed a man of God—but a severely conflicted one."

By now, we all were virtually shadows in the dusk. Eve stood directly behind me, lightly clasping my right arm. My enemy faced us, while Hugh, a few paces to his left, was reaching into his pocket, but I hurried over to him and caught his hand before he could draw out his dagger.

"Trust me," he said. "We are in no danger."

"Indeed?" The priest aimed his stick at Eve, who was no longer blocked by my body.

"Frankenstein, no!" I entreated him. (How strange to address him thus, now that I claimed his family name.) "If you must be revenged, kill me. I deserve your rancour."

"No!" he retorted. "I have had many opportunities to shoot you. But that would almost be a reward, for you do not fear death; I think you would welcome it. Revenge requires suffering. Killing you is *not enough!*"

"Nothing will ever be enough," I told him sadly. "Believe me, Frankenstein, I know. I have suffered, you know how much—but blood will never right injuries or bring back the dead. You may not wish to hear this, my poor conflicted confessor, but you and I have much in common. Your brother counted you of lesser worth; he abandoned me altogether."

With a cry and a curse, he flung his weapon to the ground, forgetting in his passion that without it to steady him, he would lose his balance and pitch forward on his face. I prevented that from happening. Holding him with one hand, I picked up his stick and, ignoring Hugh's protest, returned it to him.

Steadying himself, he shook his head in surprise and awe. "I am, perhaps," he said, "not quite so direly compromised, after all, for you have taken to heart my counsel, difficult though it was for me to give it to you. Despite your past predisposition to rage and violence, instead of injuring me, you give me back my prop, dangerous though you know it to be. Perhaps in the eyes of Heaven, the redemption you have sought is yours."

"Father," I said, clutching his arm, "let the horror end! Execute me, if you will, but do no harm to this child."

"Damn you," he growled, shaking off my hand, "I spoke just now as a priest, but I am *still your enemy!*"

Searing pain suddenly attacked. I clutched my ribs and doubled over.

"What's wrong?" he demanded.

"Chest pressure—can't breathe!" I gasped. "Pain!"

He asked where it hurt. I struck the center of my chest with my middle fingers, then ran them up to a spot beneath my jaw. Wincing with the agony of his own sciatica, he shoved me to the ground, straddled me and, clasping his hands into a doubled fist, smote my chest. Hugh's outraged yell drowned out the moan that escaped my lips. He struck a second time, a third, then Hugh, shouting "Villain!", tore him off and threw him to the ground. But the pressure and the pain in my chest were gone. I could breathe again.

"Hugh," I said, "don't hurt him!"

"No? He hit you hard enough to break your ribs!"

Eve found her way to me and knelt beside me on the grass. "Are y ' all right?"

"Yes." I sat up. "He saved my life. Give him back his stick." Hugh did so reluctantly.

Groggily rising, he shook his head in self-astonishment. "'Do no harm'—I took that oath many years ago. Apparently, it still holds power over me." Turning to me, he said, "If you return to Edinburgh, perhaps Knox can help you."

"You mean, the pain will return?"

"I have been out of practice too long, I cannot say."

"You who have so long sought revenge … why do you now try to save my life?"

"Hate the sin, but not the sinner," Frankenstein replied. "Despite myself, I am ruled by the oaths that I have taken. But do not mistake me. In the eyes of Heaven you may have redeemed yourself, but to me you are and always shall remain—*a monster.*"

He spoke no more, but, turning his back on me, limped off in the direction of Birnam Wood. I watched him till he was lost in darkness and distance.

EPILOGUE

Sacrificial

I do not know how long my heart may be able to function, but I suspect that I do not have much remaining time. I have, of course, seriously considered Ernest Frankenstein's advice that I ought to seek out Doctor Knox's counsel and expertise, but for me to return to Edinburgh would surely be fraught with risk to my freedom. We keep hearing reports that they are still seeking me further and further north of the city for the admitted murder of Henry Clerval and the deaths of Major Weir and Deacon Brodie.

I had rather not spend whatever time is left in a cold and grimy prison cell, but if they did succeed in incarcerating me, I think it doubtful that I would live long enough to end up on the gallows.

I wrote the above words some days ago. To my surprise now, and with a conjoined mixture of dismay and hope, it has been determined that I will, after all, return to Edinburgh, for Doctor Knox has written to me, and what he had to impart has formed in me a resolve to risk the dangers that await me there. I do so because of the possible good that I may be instrumental in bringing about.

Eve, the Professor and Hugh will be my travelling companions in this new adventure. I have, however, pointed out to them that if I am captured by the authorities, they might also be deemed my accomplices. Predictably, they all agreed that they were resolved to take their chances.

Just as I did the first time I rode to Edinburgh, I donned a long, cowled cloak that concealed my features. We travelled in a private coach that bore me, the Professor, Eve and Hugh the fifty-some miles that lay between Pitlochry (I had joined them there, of course, after we left Dunkeld) and Auld Reekie—so very well named! For even at night one could taste the gritty output of hundreds of coal stoves in one's mouth with the air one half-breathed, half-choked upon. We journeyed, of course, at night.

By common agreement, we decided that we must disembark some distance away from our true destination, so we selected a spot close to the Mercat Cross, a venerable monument that stands a few yards to the east of St. Giles Cathedral. From there, huddled into a close group we walked over to Surgeon's Square.

It was quite late, and the streets were mercifully deserted. The weather, for a welcome change, was mild and cool. When we got there, Hugh went on ahead into the alley-way that led to the basement of Doctor Knox's establishment. He knocked. Andrew opened the door, which was a relief. Had Paterson been on duty, we said we would have to find somewhere to stay for the rest of the night, and try again the next evening.

Hugh spoke briefly with Andrew, then he stepped back to the street end of the alley-way and beckoned to us. We joined him and went into the house, I being the last to enter. When Andrew saw me, he actually stepped up to me and shook my hand. "Doctor K. and I have been ever so worried about you! I am glad to see that you are well."

"Thank you." Truthfully, I was a bit embarrassed at his uncharacteristic (for a Scot) display of emotion. "I am not all that well, though."

"I will call Doctor K. at once!" Which meant, I suppose, that he had been told to do so, and it struck me that tonight Doctor Knox was not entertaining distaff company. Andrew hurried out; he returned shortly afterward and ushered us upstairs and into the office, where I noticed on the desk-top the physician's chess-board set up with his near-impossible mate-in-one problem.

Doctor Knox appeared quite soon after. He gave curt nods to my three companions, then, focusing his attention on me, said, "I daresay that by now you have worked out your enemy's identity, motive, and machinations?"

I grimly inclined my head, but said nothing, for I was unsure whether Eve or Hugh had told the Professor the truth about Father Naman y clept Father Dolorosa, alias Ernest Frankenstein.

The physician held out a folded scrap of paper. "I thought that you might wish to read this. It was the message that was handed to me on the night that you first arrived at my surgery."

I took it from him, unfolded it, and read about the promise of a great sum of money that would be promptly forthcoming if Doctor Knox would accept me as his patient. The missive informed him that I was a wholly manufactured creature invested with life by a scientist named Victor Frankenstein, "whom you may possibly recollect in connection with that business some years back when a body of a man by the name of Henry Clerval was discovered murdered in Ireland."

The message's final sentence clutched my heart like a cold fist: "Do all within your power to cure him of his afflictions, but the promised sum depends on fulfillment of one crucial condition, and that is that you must not in any manner or fashion anaesthetize the patient."

I gave the paper back to him. "Keep it or burn it. I have done with—all of that." I had meant to say "done with him," but, thinking that the Professor still might not be adding up the evidence against "Father Naman," I opted for less specific diction.

He tossed it into a desk drawer. "I will keep it, I think, as a memento of my most unusual case." He smiled at me with a degree of warmth that I never would have expected could exist within his brusque, self-interested spirit. "I do not know all that has transpired since the last time we were in this room together, but I do gather that you have managed to work everything out on your own."

But before I could decide how to respond, or, more to the point, change the subject, Hugh cut in. "Does that surprise you then, Doctor K.? Remember that y'r talkin' to a man who survived a blast of lightning that would have killed the both of us! Maybe that had something to do with it, but he actually solved y'r bloody mate-in-one slap-in-the-face to all existing chess masters!"

That provoked the broadest smile I had ever witnessed upon the tightly controlled physiognomy of Doctor Robert Knox. "You solved it? *Tell me!*"

I glanced at the chess-board. There they were: five pieces in this arrangement:

Black rook (or castle) in the upper left corner.
Black king one square directly below the black rook.
White pawn one square to the right of the black king.
White rook one square to the right of the white pawn.
White king two squares underneath the white pawn.

"There is only one possible move," I stated.

"That is true," the physician agreed. "Which one is it, and where does it move to?"

"The white pawn must be advanced to the top row, which puts it one square to the right of the black rook." I repositioned the white pawn on the doctor's chess-board.

"Yes," Doctor Knox nodded, "that is the correct move, and now that the white pawn has been advanced to the last row, you may exchange it for whatever you like—a queen, a bishop, rook, or knight. You could even let it stay a pawn, but after all, what difference does it make? True, you have opened up the black king to check from the white rook, but what is to stop him from moving up one diagonal square and taking the white pawn, or whatever you have changed it to?"

"If," I said, "the black king could not do that, he would have nowhere else to move because the only two remaining squares open to him are guarded by the white king. Without anywhere else for the black king to go, he will be check-mated by the white rook."

He nodded. "True, but how can you stop the black king from taking the white pawn?"

"By exchanging the white pawn for a *black* piece, it does not really matter which."

Till now, Professor MacMorris had stayed out of the conversation, but now he exclaimed, "You canna do that! I do not see the chess-board all that clearly, but I know the game well enough to follow what ye've been talkin' aboot, and I am certain that such a move is illegal! How can you change a white piece into a black one?"

"By doing it, Abel," Doctor Knox replied. "There is absolutely nothing in the international rules of chess that prevent a player from doing what our large friend has just proposed. And in this problem, it is the only possible solution."[1]

Later, in the basement surgery, I was finally alone with Doctor Knox. Well, no—Andrew was there, too, trying to make himself inconspicuous, now that the physician's examination was done. The room was as I had last seen it, save that the screen in the corner was gone.

"I regret to inform you," said the doctor, "that you have indeed suffered what is commonly called a heart attack."

"But with Ernest Frankenstein's swift aid," I said, "I managed to survive."

"That was then," he replied. "You may not be so fortunate next time."

"So it could happen again?"

"I am afraid that it is not only possible, but—probable." He put both hands to his temples. "It is late and I have a head-ache."

"Is my condition treatable?"

"Perhaps. It would require harvesting of a compatible organ in—" He coughed. "—in the usual fashion. But although it is theoretically possible to transplant a new heart into your chest, it has never yet been done. I do declare with no false modesty that if anyone might succeed in such a procedure, it would be yours truly. Still, under the most optimal of circumstances, it would be an under-taking fraught with risk."

I began to reply, but he held up his hand to stave off whatever comment I was about to make. "You need not remind me that in a matter of life or death, the only true consideration is the time that one might lose if the operation failed, whereas it is possible that you might survive for an indeterminate, yet perhaps extensive life if you were to take great care to live in a fashion that was as free from stress as possible. And you are, of course, used to taking risks. So ultimately this must be your choice ... do you want me to seek to obtain a functionable heart for you?"

There comes a time in this (what shall I call it?) sad star-adventure,

---

1   See Afterword for details.

when one must think of others, not oneself. This was such a time.

"Tell me, Doctor Knox," I said, "have you looked into the problem of optics that we discussed some time back?"

He nodded. "Not only have I retrained myself in optical surgery, I have studied those astonishing note-books that catalogue the researches, insights, and procedures of Victor Frankenstein."

"All very well," I replied, "but what about Eve?"

"I note from the more than usual harshness of your voice that you wish an answer from me, not a protracted discussion. Very well. I have known the MacMorris girl ever since she was born. Her condition was inherited from her mother, but I believe her organs of sight are not irrevocably damaged, but structurally compromised, and therefore theoretically repairable. However … "

"Go on!"

Fingering the diamond stick-pin in his colourful ascot, Doctor Knox sighed. "Let me reassure you that I am wholly committed to this business, but the procedure I envision is rife with enormous difficulties, and much as I detest admitting it, I lack extensive experience as an optical surgeon."

"Would she be endangered by the procedure?"

"Every operation, no matter how minor, carries potential risk. But that is not the reason that I hesitate."

He was trying my temper, and he knew it, but I made myself stay calm as I asked him what the real problem was.

"*Eyes!*" he declared. "Of all harvestable organs, they are among the swiftest to decay and lose their function."

I regarded this as useful information, for it suggested something altogether different to me than what it must have imported to Doctor Knox. I told him what I was prepared to do.

His eyes widened. "Yes, that might work—but you know what that would mean!"

"Yes," I growled. "Do it while I still am capable of functioning, and before I have second thoughts…"

(Eve MacMorris)

If I had any idea what Willie had in mind, I never would have agreed to it. But the only thing that Doctor Knox told me was that he had found a satisfactory organ donor and it was not necessary to replace my eyes, for he said he could not hope to succeed in doing that, but there were certain tissues that might be switched. He warned me that it might not work, and reminded me of the risks inherent in any sort of surgery, but I did not believe I would end up any worse off than I was already, so I determined to go through with it, which took some effort to convince my father, but at last he assented, and so I was operated on, and it was a smashing success!

I can *see!*—but at such a price!

For though the doctor would not tell us the name of the tissue donor, we all meant to take Willie back to Pitlochry where he would be safer than in Edinburgh. Well, it did not take us long to realize that it was he who had sacrificed his own eye-sight for me.

◖ ❦ ◗

O, what a riot of colours and forms and things to examine and touch and study. My own father's face, which I had never ever seen! My dear brother Hugh—what a good-looking lad! Much different than his brisk, gruff voice led me to expect.

But Willie—! O, Willie!

Doctor Knox's assistant Andrew Napier had loaned him his room to recuperate. Willie was asleep when I visited him, but he woke as I walked into his bed-chamber. He knew it was me at once, and he groaned. "I had wished to spare you from seeing my ugliness."

I pretended to scold him. "Now, listen to me, y' hear? This business of seeing is a great new thing to me, but I have my own mind and my own set o' values, and no one, do y' hear, *no one* is going to tell me what is good to look upon and what is ugly t' behold. Willie, Willie, with every wee bit o' joy I feel this moment because of you, my sweet guardian angel, I declare that to me you always ha' been and always will be—*beautiful.*"

When one's heart is breaking, sometimes the only thing to do is to make a joke out of it. "An' if y' dinna wish me t' look at y', Willie, y' certainly had a strange way of going about it!"

Sometimes when he used to read to me, there would be a funny passage and on those rare occasions, I would hear a hoarse kind of rasp that was his way of laughing. I heard that sound comin' from him now, but like me, his mirth was mixed with tears.

Later on that day, I walked about town in awe of all the lovely sights and gaudy spectacles of life in a great city that I now could see. Yes, I also saw a great deal of dinginess, but even that had his fascination. But my ears are still particularly keen, and so when I returned, I told my father and my brother that I had heard talk about the search for the West Port "giant", that the authorities meant to scour Scotland to find him, and by now searchers were at Pitlochry, where they were scouring the woods because someone had told them that that is where their prey had hid himself. So much for Robbie Pratt keeping his mouth shut!

Me and my father and brother all went down to Andrew's room to warn Willie about what I had heard. But we found him in no further danger, for he had died in his sleep. Doctor Knox joined us presently and after he did a brief examination, he said that a second heart attack was responsible for his death, "but, at least," he said, "it was mercifully swift. I am sure that he did not suffer."

Eventually, I examined the great sheaf of papers that he had written about the latter passages of his life. (First, of course, I had to learn how to read and write, but I did so with great rapidity, for I was, as you may imagine, quite motivated, partly for my own sake, and partly so that I could entertain and solace my father by reading to him, as he did to me when I was a little girl.)

Even with those speculative chapters that Willie had written from other view-points, his story had its share of missing details, and therefore, over time, I filled in a few of the lacunae by writing, albeit unwillingly, to Ernest Frankenstein, who graciously, I must admit, supplied information that let me contribute to this tale those chapters prefaced by this symbol—*(?)*

One more thing that I need to tell you—when we went down to Andrew's bed-chamber and found that our friend had died, I found upon the floor near his unclasped hand a last scrap of paper that he had written upon.

Doctor Knox read it aloud so that all of us could hear and share Willie's final thoughts, and here they are—

In my breast I sense an erratic rhythm. This huge,

ungainly frame that Victor Frankenstein stitched together and shocked into life is breaking down, at last. Tomorrow and tomorrow and tomorrow, and I shall be no more. My thoughts keep returning to those early days when I thought that my future might be bright with promise. But this faltering sinner, no longer innocent, will leave the world unloved.

No, that is not true. Eve, the Professor and Hugh all truly care for me, and this is a consolation that sweetens Death's bitter sting. Still, I have known too much of cruelty and sin, and even their simple decency, and the counsels of Father Naman, cannot wholly cleanse my infected spirit.

My spirit—yes, I am somehow sure of its existence, though nothing but mine own desire to be accounted a complete and independent entity makes me think so. Yet dear Professor MacMorris once told me that there is such a thing as intuitive wisdom that we must learn to recognize and accept, and mine maintains that I do possess something whose nature is immortal. Does that mean that my misdeeds on earth have earned me an eternal place in Hell? I do not think that a merciful deity would allow everlasting torment for sins committed out of loneliness and despair, but if there is such a personage as "God," which I still doubt, consider the nature of the world he is said to have fashioned, and upon doing so, ask if it is likely to find such a creator merciful. I only know that if unending punishment awaits me in another sphere, life has already taught me much of its character.

O, Father (I dare to call you that)—when you lay dying in Captain Walton's ship, I heard you tell him that you owed me more than you ever gave. But now that I approach mine own ending, I think that sons must learn to forgive their progenitors for not being gods, and this is a lesson that I have learned, Victor Frankenstein, from your own brother, Ernest.

I hope, my only Creator, that if you still possess consciousness on some plane of existence, you no longer curse me. I seek your forgiveness, and I freely give you mine, for, despite the stubborn promptings of my not-wholly dying heart, I must and shall try at last to love you.

Your only son,

FRANKENSTEIN

AFTERWORD

with Historical Notes & Acknowledgments

On the Problems of Mysteries and Pastiche

The Passion of Frankenstein had an odd inception, growth and delivery. In earlier incarnations, it was called *A Race of Monsters*, and before that, its title was, simply, *Frankenstein, Detective*. The reason it began with such a title is that some years ago, Don Maass, who had long been my literary agent, sold what is known in the trade as a "high concept" mystery series, for which its author received an uncommonly generous advance against royalties. Don suggested that I should devise such a series that he would submit to the same publisher.

Now mysteries and I are old acquaintances, if not friends. Personally, I have always preferred reading—and writing and editing—in the fantasy/science fiction genre, as well as play scripts. I invested my academic years in the performing arts, holding two degrees in theatre and English literature. Now the late Professor Ellis Grove, a dear friend of mine at Penn State, once gave me the splendid gift of a huge assortment of issues of *Ellery Queen Mystery Magazine*, since destroyed, along with much of my book collection, in a flood at Kingston, Pennsylvania. At any rate, those old EQMM's provided a rich education for me in the classic mystery story; before then the only mysteries I read were the Sherlock Holmes tales and the amusing H. M. series by Carter Dickson (John Dickson Carr). David Ossar, a college roommate, got me hooked on Rex Stout, and only a few other mystery writers ever got my attention afterward— Anthony Boucher, Leslie Charteris, Dick Francis, Dashiell Hammett, Leonard Holton (mentioned below), Leo Perutz (not principally a genre writer), Clayton Rawson, Hake Talbot (Henning Nelms)—it is a very short list.

Yet my professional involvement in the mystery genre has been, to me, surprisingly extensive. Not only did I write seven novels, a few short shorts, and one novella, I taught my plotting system for more than twenty years at New York University, and have a goodly roster of students who went on to become published writers, including, among others, Shannon Cork, George Cronin, Kara George, Rachel Mann, Dianne Neral, Kathleen Snow, Triss Stein, Carolyn Wheat. I've served as judge for the Edgar, Nero and International Thriller Writer Awards, spent many weeks in England as a lecturer for the Smithsonian Institute, speaking on British mystery writers at the English places they were associated with. Currently, I am editor of *Sherlock Holmes Mystery Magazine,* as well as *Weird Tales.*

Despite these credentials, my taste for the whodunit has become further alienated over the years because the nature of today's novels is quite different from those created during what Ellery Queen called the Golden Age and John Dickson Carr referred to as The Grandest Game. Today's mysteries are mostly crime novels, but are seldom the reader-solvable puzzles that used to define the term. Why is this so? Probably because the classic whodunit is an exceedingly difficult form to devise; it is perhaps similar to the fugue: one may follow all of the demanding rules and end up with a well-constructed fugue that also is a very uninteresting work of music; the same pertains to the classic whodunit.

So when my agent proposed that I devise a "high concept" mystery series, I did so reluctantly, given my personal ambivalence to the form. What I came up with was the idea of a series of novels, each of which involved a famous literary character as the protagonist-raissoneur—i.e., the detective. The first one would be the Frankenstein monster, for I have always considered Mary Shelley's novel one of the finest masterpieces of English letters; another detective would have been Jane Eyre, for the same reason just stated, and a third would have been Ebenezer Scrooge, whom I have already written about in my previous novel, *The Last Christmas of Ebenezer Scrooge* (Wildside Press), and who I planned to have solve Dickens's *The Mystery of Edwin Drood.*

None of this came about as planned. As I began writing the Frankenstein novel, plotting problems surfaced. The story insisted on dictating a different shape involving character interplay, which too often is compacted by the structural needs of the classic mystery.

Over the period of several years, I abandoned and returned to the problem until Don, my agent, finally suggested that I stop trying to write a mystery and focus, instead, on a pastiche subsequent to the events of Mary Shelley's classic novel.

I gladly took Don's advice, and at last the book began to take life for me, and though *The Passion of Frankenstein*, in its final guise, is free from the Procrustean rigours of mystery plotting, perversely, some elements of the whodunit found their way into it, after all.

In shaping what I hope to be a moderately plausible continuation of *Frankenstein*, I am aware of and concerned by the demands of literary pastiche. Now the dictionary defines pastiche as a jumbled hodgepodge of artistic elements, whether artistic, literary, or musical, but that is not the usage it has taken on in the world of *belles lettres*. Unlike the mocking nature of parody, pastiche is intended as a respectful re-creation of an author's diction, plotting, and style.

When I wrote my sequel to *A Christmas Carol,* it was not difficult to emulate the Dickensian model; often I found it advisable to simplify the diction of the original for the benefit of the contemporary reader, but this could be accomplished without wholly sacrificing the syntactical Dickensian flow. This proved to be a greater problem, however, in *The Passion of Frankenstein.* Mary Shelley's narrative style proved easy enough to emulate, but considerable editorial pruning and simplification seemed necessary to me when employing the creature's narrative voice. Those who have not read *Frankenstein* and rely on their knowledge of the tale from its various cinematic representations really do not know very much about it. Only the Kenneth Branagh film follows the novel with any consistency, though it also takes its own share of liberties. One of the most striking surprises in the book is the creature's quasi-Biblical apostrophes and declamations as he tells his story for six hefty chapters! I have tried to retain a modest amount of this voicing to stay true to that element of the Mary Shelley original, but the creature in *The Passion of Frankenstein* is definitely more laconic.

Historical Notes

Dating is as close to historical accuracy as is necessary for a work of fantasy. Though both the 1818 and more familiar later edition of *Frankenstein* were consulted, neither sets the action's precise years, but it is close enough to certain Edinburgh doings to believe it reasonable that Burke, Hare and Knox were in business long before their enterprise became public.

Doctor Knox, William Burke and Willie Hare are all drawn from contemporary accounts of their respective characters. Doctor Knox did indeed serve in the military in Belgium and Africa. We know less about Helen MacDougal, and she was acquitted from any culpability in the West Port murders, but that verdict is generally believed to be a matter more of luck than deserts.

Andrew Napier is invented, but Doctor Knox did employ a janitor named David Paterson. Nothing much is known about him, though it has been speculated that he was involved in receiving cadavers from the Resurrectionists. Patsy Kensit is also invented, though her complaint about "Pope-songs" was borrowed from an incident that happened at an Edinburgh church a long time ago.

The original Deacon Brodie was hanged before Frankenstein came to Edinburgh. He did have children, but there is no evidence to show that any of them followed in their father's footsteps.

There really was a Daft Jamie, and it is generally believed that Burke or Hare killed him, though in fact it happened subsequent to the events of this tale. His snuff-box was brass, not silver. The details of his mother throwing him out of her house, and his subsequent begging, and popularity with the citizenry, are all true.

Mary Tennant also was one of Burke and Hare's victims. The shock of her turning up in the operating theatre has been used to considerable melodramatic advantage in films.

If one takes one of the several tourist "ghost walks" available in Edinburgh, guides will assure you that Burke and Hare were not "body-snatchers" because they would never have been permitted into that union. When the pair were finally arrested for murder,

Lord Advocate Sir William Rae offered Hare immunity if he turned King's evidence against Burke. Hare and his wife sent Burke to death by hanging on January 28th, 1829, though Burke's mistress, Helen MacDougall, escaped because the jury declared that the charges against her had not been proved. When Burke was cut down from the gallows, many Edinburgh citizens reportedly stood in line to purchase bits of flesh for turning into purses and other memorabilia. The city's Surgeon's Hall Museum still displays a large book covered with tanned skin from Burke's buttocks, and the University of Edinburgh owns his skeleton.

Hare is said to have died penniless in London in 1859. Knox never was legally implicated, but animosity against him became so great that he eventually relocated to London.

The broadside displayed in the Part II chapter titled "The Power of the Press" is modeled closely in type faces and style to ones printed in Edinburgh at the time of the West Port murders.

The blind woman's death was suggested by an incident in Val Lewton's great 1945 horror film, *The Body Snatcher*, which was based on a story of the same name by Robert Louis Stevenson, who clearly had Burke, Hare and Knox in mind when he wrote it.

Stevenson, of course, also drew on Edinburgh's dark history for his famous novella, *The Strange Case of Doctor Jekyll and Mr. Hyde*, which was his "take" on the Deacon Brodie who supposedly fathered the character in this novel. At one point in this narrative, a local writer is cited as terming Edinburgh's weather as "treacherous," and that was also Robert Louis Stevenson.

Major Weir's home is patterned on Lady Stair's House, site of a famous Edinburgh ghost story set down by Sir Walter Scott as "The Tale of the Mysterious Mirror." Today, this house is a museum devoted to three Scottish authors, with one floor apiece dedicated to Scott, Stevenson, and Robert Burns. Major Weir is an incarnation of an earlier personage of that name known as "the Wizard of the West Bow," who was indeed burned as a self-confessed wizard, along with his sister/lover.

The spiritualist Porteous, though fictional, is loosely based on a seer who, despite religious disapproval, was often sought for readings by Edinburgh gentry; this seer and his mirror were modeled after the mage in Scott's factual/fictional mirror story mentioned above.

In the first chapter of Part Two, Andrew Napier describes Edinburgh's many-storied "lands," which were the historic predecessors of modern skyscrapers, and muses that "Someday, I fear, fire will sweep it all away. Perhaps only then could we build a cleaner, purer city." A catastrophic fire indeed destroyed much of the Royal Mile and Old Town in November, 1824. The new section of town that Andrew Napier states was being contemplated was indeed built north of the moat, which was drained and replaced with grass and flowers. It is said that when it was drained, some six thousand bodies were found in it.

I did not find any evidence to prove whether Doctor Knox was or was not a chess player. The checkmate-in-one problem is borrowed from a later chess master: Ksawery Tarkatower, who was known in English as Savielly Tarkatower. He was a Polish and French Grandmaster, and was born in 1887. Tarkatower became the world's leading chess journalist during the 1920's and 1930s. Tarkatower was noted for his aphoristic wit and brilliant gamesmanship. According to Tony Corinda, in his book, *13 Steps to Mentalism*, one day Tarkatower walked into a London chess club and challenged everyone to solve a mate in one problem. The notion seemed ridiculous; one needn't be a chess master to work out how to win in *one* move—only no one was able to do it.

We do not know whether Tarkatower's solution annoyed them, but I suspect it did because the rules of international chess eventually were amended to render his strategy illegal. But in the time frame of *The Passion of Frankenstein*, Tarkatower's bold ploy would have been perfectly permissible.

Doctor Usui, who taught the priest how to do hands-on healing is named after Doctor Mikao Usui, founder of Reiki Ryoho Gakkai, the reiki system in whose lineage I trained nine steps down from Doctor Usui. Though the research that evolved into modern reiki occurred long after the events of this novel, Doctor Usui considered it a rediscovery of old principles long practiced by Buddhist monks. Acupuncture, of course, as represented by Doctor Knox's needles, is an extremely venerable Asian medical discipline.

Acknowledgments

In addition to the two editions of Mary (& Percy, in the later and better known version) Shelley's *Frankenstein, or The Modern*

Prometheus, to which is added internet research, my chief bibliographical sources include the *Edinburgh Street Guide* (John Bartholomew & Son Ltd., 1988, Edinburgh); *Burke & Hare: The Resurrection Men,* edited by Jacques Barzun (The Scarecrow Press, 1974, Metuchen, New Jersey); *Scottish Hauntings* by Grant Campbell (Piccolo/Pan Books, 1982, London); *The True Story of Burke & Hare* by John Mackay (Lang Syne Publishers Ltd., no year declared, Glasgow); *Adam Lyal's Witchery Tales* by Colin MacPhail and Robin Mitchell (Moubray House Press, 1988, Edinburgh); *Haunted Edinburgh* by Rupert Matthews (Pitkin Pictorials Limited, 1993, Hampshire, Great Britain); *Ghostly Scotland* by Lily Seafield (Geddes & Grosset, 2006, New Lanark, Scotland), and *Ghosts and Ghouls in Historic Edinburgh* by Alan J. Wilson, Des Brogan and Frank McGrail (Edinburgh Impressions Ltd., 1989, Edinburgh).

The name that the creature nearly chooses for himself, William Henry Pratt, was the real name of Boris Karloff.

Researchers need not waste time looking for the "obscure French philosopher" who allegedly penned the aphorism, *All things without a name are evil,* that so depressed the creature in the first chapter written from his viewpoint. The writer and the quote are pure fantasy, as is the writer Graëbeck, mentioned in the chapter with the title, *A Private Arrangement.*

The name of Dunkeld's spiritual leader, Father Joseph Bredder, is an authorial tribute to the detective-hero of a splendid series of novels by the pseudonymous Leonard Holton, whose true identity was Leonard Wibberly, author of the delightful novel, *The Mouse that Roared.*

The phrase, "sad star-adventure," that the creature employs near the close of his story is an echo of part of a closing speech in Maxwell Anderson's play, *Winterset.*

I consulted three British film representations of the West Port murders: *Burke & Hare (1972),* an engagingly lurid film starring the estimable Harry Andrews as Doctor Knox; *The Doctor and the Devils* (1985), with Timothy Dalton as Knox and costarring Jonathan Pryce, Twiggy (!), Beryl Reid, Stephen Rea, and Patrick Stewart, with a revised version of a 1940 screenplay by no less than Dylan Thomas, and easily the best of this cinematic trio—*Flesh and the Fiends* (1959) featuring a spectacular cast: Peter Cushing as Knox, George Rose as Burke and Donald Pleasance as Hare. This version, closest to the true story, though it does take its share of speculative liberties, contains two of the ugliest murders I have ever seen in the movies.

Thanks to Carole Buggé, my dear friend and colleague (and this book's dedicatee), for bringing me back all sorts of lore and an authentic Edinburgh cap to wear when she was away during her residency at the Hawthorden Castle Retreat for Writers, in Lasswade, Scotland.

Thanks to Donald Maass for suggesting certain significant elements of the plot.

Special thanks to my friend and fellow author Kathleen C. Szaj for help concerning vital aspects of the plot, particularly in reference to the spiritual conflict of its antagonist.

Thanks to Pat LoBrutto, friend and editor of five of my books, for reading *The Passion of Frankenstein* and offering cogent advice for one important revision.

Thanks to Doctor Harry M. Engel for suggestions appertaining to eye surgery.

Details concerning the creature's latter physical concerns are derived from the Standardized Patient work that I do at the Morchand Center of Mt. Sinai Hospital, the Clinical Competence Center of New York, and Kaplan Medical, in Newark, New Jersey.

Thanks to the staffs and management of three of my favorite Upper West Side Manhattan restaurants, Café Eighty-Two, Sushi Hana (now called Amaze), and The Parlour, where, in homage to Scotland, with the aid of wee drams of Ballantine's, Famous Grouse, and Johnnie Walker Black, I completed most of the latter chapters of this book.

And thanks, finally, if belatedly, to my gracious hosts during my visits to Pitlochry, Doctor Trevor Ross and his wife, my high school chum Margo Sheldon Ross, who first led me through Dunkeld Cathedral and showed me its monolith, which Margo described to me as "just as old as Stonehenge, but we Scots don't fence it off so you can't touch it!", as well as the leper's crawl (squint), and the sarcophagus of "the Wolf of Dudenach," all of which also found a place in my novella, "The Haunted Single Malt," which appeared in the

2008 Tor Books anthology, *The Ghost Quartet*. Dunkeld Cathedral's dating in the text is accurate, but its architecture may be somewhat less so, inasmuch as I visited it over two decades ago, and have no photos of it.

—Marvin Kaye
New York City